W9-CCE-843

"Roger, why haven't you ever remarried?"

Violet asked as she gazed into the fire.

"Are you proposing to me?" A mischievous twinkle sparkled in his dark eyes.

"Of course not," she said. "I'm just…curious. Don't you miss sharing your life with someone?"

"At first the pain was too deep to even consider it. But lately, I have been thinking about marrying again," he admitted.

Roger stood and stoked the fire. "Now it's my turn to ask questions—are you going to marry Larry Holland?"

His question startled her, but she smiled. "He hasn't asked me."

"But if he does, will you marry him?" Roger continued to look at her, his gaze intense.

Violet looked away. She stared into the flames.

"I've often asked myself the same question. Right now, I honestly don't know.…"

Books by Irene Brand

Love Inspired

Child of Her Heart #19
Heiress #37
To Love and Honor #49

IRENE BRAND

This prolific and popular author of both contemporary and historical inspirational fiction is a native of West Virginia, where she has lived all her life. She began writing professionally in 1977, after she completed her master's degree in history at Marshall University. Irene taught in secondary public schools for twenty-three years, but retired in 1989 to devote herself full-time to her writing.

In 1984, after a long career of publishing articles and devotional materials, her first novel was published by Thomas Nelson. Since that time, Irene has published fourteen contemporary and historical novels and three nonfiction titles with publishers such as Zondervan, Fleming Revell and Barbour Books.

Her extensive travels with her husband, Rod, to forty-nine of the United States and twenty-four foreign countries have inspired much of her writing. Through her writing, Irene believes she has been helpful to others, and is grateful to the many readers who have written to say that her truly inspiring stories and compelling portrayals of characters of strong faith have made a positive impression on their lives.

To Love and Honor
Irene Brand

Love Inspired

Published by Steeple Hill Books™

If you purchased this book without a cover you should be aware that this book is stolen property. It was reported as "unsold and destroyed" to the publisher, and neither the author nor the publisher has received any payment for this "stripped book."

STEEPLE HILL BOOKS

Steeple
Hill™

ISBN 0-373-87049-3

TO LOVE AND HONOR

Copyright © 1999 by Irene Brand

All rights reserved. Except for use in any review, the reproduction or utilization of this work in whole or in part in any form by any electronic, mechanical or other means, now known or hereafter invented, including xerography, photocopying and recording, or in any information storage or retrieval system, is forbidden without the written permission of the editorial office, Steeple Hill Books, 300 East 42nd Street, New York, NY 10017 U.S.A.

All characters in this book have no existence outside the imagination of the author and have no relation whatsoever to anyone bearing the same name or names. They are not even distantly inspired by any individual known or unknown to the author, and all incidents are pure invention.

This edition published by arrangement with Steeple Hill Books.

® and TM are trademarks of Steeple Hill Books, used under license. Trademarks indicated with ® are registered in the United States Patent and Trademark Office, the Canadian Trade Marks Office and in other countries.

Printed in U.S.A.

For I was hungry and you gave me something to eat, I was thirsty and you gave me something to drink, I was a stranger and you invited me in, I needed clothes and you clothed me, I was sick and you looked after me, I was in prison and you came to visit me.

—*Matthew* 25:35-36

...I was hungry, and you gave me something to
eat; I was thirsty, and you gave me something to
drink; I was a stranger, and you invited me in; I had
no clothes, and you clothed me; I was sick, and
you looked after me; I was in prison, and you came
to visit me.

—Matthew 25:35-36

Chapter One

As the closing school bell rang, Violet Conley dropped into her teacher's chair with a deep sigh. Would she ever sponsor another Social Studies Fair? She closed her eyes for a few minutes, and then opened them slowly. Did the room really look as bad as she had thought?

Afraid so! Violet conceded grimly, as she pushed herself upward. She had permitted the students to work too late in their frenzy to be ready by the weekend, and they hadn't had time to clean up the classroom before catching their buses. All of them were gone except Janie Skeen, who was shelving books. Janie lived two blocks from the school, so she often stayed behind to help Violet. The girl's slender body already exhibited lovely curves and grace, and except for the melancholy look in her deep brown, long-lashed eyes, she would have been beautiful.

Violet was pleased to have Janie's help, for the whole room was in disarray, due to the past several days of research. While valuable to the pupils, it had been hard on a teacher's nerves.

"You're probably glad that tomorrow is the last day to work on projects," Janie said with a slight smile.

"Right now, that's true," Violet agreed as she carried the waste bin from desk to desk picking up litter. "But when the projects are all arranged, and I see the culminated effort of our whole school, I forget about the frustration and hard work." She shook her head in exasperation as she picked up a book that a student had left behind, for it was a book on the rules of football, which he undoubtedly was reading when he should have been working on his class assignment. She locked the book in her desk. She would discover, and admonish, the culprit when he came looking for his book.

"You say your project is coming along well?"

"Yes, I think so," Janie said timidly, "but I don't suppose I'll be a winner."

"You'll have as much chance as anyone." When Janie still looked skeptical, Violet added, "The judges are from out of town, so names won't mean anything to them."

No need to pretend that she didn't know the reason behind Janie's skepticism. Janie had enrolled in Maitland High at the beginning of the school year, but she hadn't been accepted by her peers. The teachers liked Janie, because she was well behaved and eager to learn, but most of the students ignored her...some because they feared her, others considered she was inferior to themselves, while the majority of pupils didn't know how to befriend a runaway girl who had lived on the streets of Chicago for six months, before she was placed in a foster home in Maitland, their small town in southern Illinois.

Moving into the computer room, Violet found it in better shape than the classroom. The students had found the Internet indispensable in researching their projects, and Violet was happy that the principal, Larry Holland, had secured a federal grant to provide the equipment. Violet sat at one computer and typed in a password to check her E-mail. "Receiving one message of one," she read, hoping that the communication wouldn't require any further work on her part today.

"Don't forget our date. I'll pick you up at six. Larry"

The day's frustrations were forgotten and, with a broad smile on her face, Violet clicked the icon, Return to Author, and typed in "OK." On days when Violet didn't have occasion to speak privately with Larry, he often contacted her on the Internet.

Although the classroom was orderly at last, Janie loitered. "Thank you, Janie," Violet said with a warm smile. "You've been a big help, but you should go now. I'll need to leave in a few minutes."

Janie picked up her books and, with a wave of her hand, walked out into the hall, passing Nan Oliver in the doorway.

"I wish I could give that girl a big hug every day," Violet said, as her friend and fellow teacher sat at a student's desk that was much too small for her plump frame.

"I know what you mean. The girl is starved for love. I hate these new rules that forbid us to touch any of our students."

"I wonder if her foster mother is good to her."

"As far as I know, Margaret Grady is a good and caring person, but she's mothering three foster children, and since Janie is the oldest, she probably doesn't get much attention. I'm sure she has enough food, and her clothes are adequate, but she has such a lonely look in her eyes."

"She stirs my sympathy and a desire to mother her," Violet commented.

"I suppose we can never understand what it's like to grow up with a troubled childhood," Nan said. "When I remember how secure I felt at home, I can't comprehend what life has been for Janie and others like her. Can you?"

Violet lowered her eyes. Although Nan was her closest friend on the staff, there were some details about her past that she couldn't disclose even to her. Fortunately, she didn't have to answer because the all-clear buzzer sounded, indicating that the students were gone and teachers could leave the building. Nan heaved herself out of the chair.

"I'd better run," Violet said. "Larry is picking me up at six o'clock, and I have lots of things to do before then."

She locked her classroom door and walked down the hall at Nan's side.

"Heavy date, huh?"

"It's his mother's sixty-fifth birthday, and we're going to Saint Louis to celebrate. Many of her relatives live in Saint Louis, and they've reserved a private room in an exclusive restaurant."

"Must be nice to travel with the upper crust!" Nan said, her smile taking the sting from her words.

"Oh, I don't know," Violet said, lowering her

voice. "Why does she approve of me, when she's chased away the other women he's dated?"

"If you don't mind my saying so, it isn't any credit to you. She's probably decided that you aren't any threat to her, that if Larry marries you, she can still control his life. If you do anything to cross her, she'll boot you out the door in a hurry."

"In other words, you're suggesting that I'm wishy-washy," Violet accused with uplifted brows.

"Those are your words, not mine," Nan replied, and her round face exploded into laughter. Seriously, she added, "I hate to see you mixed up with that family."

"Well, I may just dare to disagree with one of Olivia Holland's opinions tonight. That will give her a reason to remember her sixty-fifth birthday. Would that suit you?"

"If you do, I may need to come to Saint Louis to bring you home, but don't expect to reach me until after the soccer game. I'm driving my boys and other team members tonight."

A ten-minute drive brought Violet to her home. She entered the house with a sigh of pleasure. Since she had bought this house a year ago, it had been a sanctuary. The four-room dwelling, a bungalow so typical of the Midwest fifty years ago, had been a bargain. Violet had spent a lot of time working on the house, painting, papering and even making window curtains.

A serving bar separated the small, convenient kitchen from the dining space. She ate her meals at the bar, and she didn't entertain much, so the dining room served as an office, where she used a computer to write her lesson plans.

Her bedroom was large, and a bathroom separated

it from the smaller bedroom, which was only big enough for a single bed. This was Aunt Ruth's room during her occasional visits to Maitland.

The living room was cozy. Bookshelves lined one wall and several easy chairs and a comfortable couch faced the television. Ruffled curtains graced the double windows that opened on the porch. A bookcase housed Violet's collection of ceramic dolls that she had been gathering since childhood. Several landscape prints hung on the cream-colored papered walls, and a multicolored carpet covered the floor. A fireplace, housing a gas stove, provided extra warmth to the house on those days when she didn't need the furnace.

After Violet went out on the porch for her mail, she decided that she had a few minutes to relax before she dressed for the evening, so she settled into the lounge chair in the living room and put her feet up.

She laid aside the two bills, pitched the junk mail into the small waste can beside her chair, and opened Aunt Ruth's letter. The note was brief, as they always were, but receiving them weekly made a big difference in Violet's life. She had always struggled with the need to establish an identity, and that was one reason she was so sympathetic to the plight of Janie Skeen. Aunt Ruth and her husband had given Violet a home from the time she was two years old, but that wasn't the same as living with one's parents. Violet had fought all her life to overcome a feeling of inadequacy, so she understood Janie's situation completely. Aunt Ruth lived alone since her husband's death five years ago, but her notes were always upbeat as she wrote about her part-time job, the neighborhood children and her church activities.

Not least among the debts that Violet owed to Aunt

Ruth was the blessing of living in a Christian home. Church attendance had been a part of Violet's upbringing, instilling a dependence upon God in her that had often been the only consolation she had during her maturing years.

Reluctantly, Violet left the cozy chair and went to the bedroom to dress for the evening. She was flattered that Larry Holland, Maitland's most eligible bachelor, had singled her out for his attention, but still she dreaded this evening. When she was alone with Larry, Violet was content, but she was always uncomfortable in Olivia Holland's company. The Hollands were rich and very influential in the state, and Mrs. Holland never let one forget the fact. Her own family had impeccable lineage, or so she insisted, and she didn't let anyone forget that, either. When they first started dating, Violet had expected Mrs. Holland to check her ancestry, but apparently she hadn't, for Violet was convinced that if the aristocratic Olivia Holland had even looked into Violet's family background, she would have heard about it.

Larry wasn't like his mother, else Violet wouldn't have given him a second glance, although he had subtly suggested a few times that Violet should buy more expensive clothes, a hint she had ignored. By the time she made payments on her house and car, she didn't have enough money to buy designer clothing.

So, what was she going to wear tonight? She soon decided on a navy, ankle-length silk skirt and long-sleeved lace blouse that matched her violet eyes—a striking feature that had resulted in her name.

Violet showered quickly, wearing a cap over her head, because she didn't have time for a shampoo and styling. Fortunately, Violet's naturally curly hair was easily managed. She visited the hairdresser to have it cut and shaped every two months, but the rest of the time a few strokes with a brush left her short hair in black soft curls all over her head.

She applied makeup sparingly. Her fine features and smooth skin, rich and deep in texture, needed little enhancement. She left off eye makeup completely, because her violet eyes fringed by long, up-curling black lashes were naturally distinctive. Violet was above average height and well proportioned. With her graceful form, even inexpensive garments set well on her.

She knew that Larry would arrive promptly at six o'clock, so she was surprised when the doorbell rang twenty minutes before that. She pulled a lightweight evening jacket from the closet and rushed to the door.

Her friend, Roger Gibson, stood on the porch. "Oh, hello," she said. "Come in."

He whistled. "Wow! You are really dolled up this evening. If you're going out, I'll come back later."

"Larry won't pick me up for fifteen minutes. Come on in."

Roger, a lieutenant in the Illinois State Police, and his family attended the same church as Violet, and he had been her friend since she had moved to Maitland. He stepped inside the living room, which seemed to shrink with the presence of his tall, powerful build. Roger was off duty now, and in casual dress, but in his policeman's uniform, Violet had often thought he looked awesome.

"Actually, I'm begging," he said. "The church youth group are sponsoring a garage sale next month, and we're looking for donations. We'll take anything that's salable."

"I'm sure I can scrounge up some good items, but

you'll have to wait for it until after the Social Studies Fair is over.''

Roger was the father of Misty Gibson, one of Violet's pupils so he knew about the fair. ''Oh, yes, I'll be happy when that event is over, so I can take possession of our dining room table again. Misty has been struggling for several days to make a papier-mâché model of the White House. Perhaps I shouldn't tell you that.''

His generous mouth with rather full lips broke into a smile, causing attractive crinkles at the corners of his dark eyes. Roger Gibson had thick dark hair, curled close to his head, with touches of silver at the temples. His dusky skin hinted of a Middle East ancestry far in the past. With his warm, open nature Roger possessed an air of decency and strong character. Violet always felt elevated to a higher spiritual and moral level when she was in his presence.

''It doesn't matter, for I won't be one of the judges. I'll give them a grade for turning in the project, but I won't have to decide which is the best one, thank goodness.''

Roger's brown eyes resembled deep dark pools when he smiled again. ''Artistic ability isn't one of Misty's strong points. I'm not concerned about having to escort her to the regional competition in Missouri.'' He moved toward the door. ''I'll go now. I see Larry driving down the street. See you at church on Sunday.''

Rather than observing Larry's approach, Violet admired Roger's energetic walk toward his truck. His step was fast and springy, an unusual gait in such a large man. A widower when Violet first met him, he bore well the responsibility of rearing two children by himself.

She turned to greet Larry when he stepped up on the porch.

"Ready on time, as usual," Larry said. Roger waved to them as he drove his pickup down the street.

"Are you in trouble?" Larry asked, smiling, but with a hint of worry in his eyes.

Pulling the door shut behind her, and taking Larry's arm as they left the porch and walked to his car, Violet said, "Oh, you mean Roger. He directs the youth activities at our church, and he was soliciting items for the group's garage sale. Roger was one of the first people I met when I moved to Maitland. He nearly gave me a ticket for neglecting to signal a right-hand turn." She laughed at the memory. "And after he let me off with a stern warning, he invited me to attend his church. We've been friends ever since."

"Not the usual way to make friends, I'd say."

"Perhaps not, but I couldn't ask for a better friend. In fact, he tries to befriend everyone."

"Have you ever considered leaving that church, Violet? It's too conservative and folksy for me. You would be welcome at the church we attend."

"But I'm welcome at First Community Church, too. The large church family I've gained there makes up for the small natural family I have."

Violet tried to keep her voice from reflecting the irritation she felt, for she suspected that Mrs. Holland was behind Larry's comments. She was ready to take issue with him, but he dropped the subject and looked at her approvingly. "May I say that you're looking fantastic tonight? Mother will be pleased."

"You look pretty sharp, too. Perhaps I'm not the

one to say this, but we do make a good-looking couple," she said, eyeing, with appreciation, his black suit, snow-white shirt, and expensive silk tie, its rich burgundy and gray pattern a perfect contrast to his dark suit.

One couldn't help admire Larry Holland. With the family wealth, he wouldn't have to work at all, yet at thirty, he had already earned his doctorate in education, and had been the principal at Maitland High for five years. His brown hair swept back from his forehead in deep waves, and his eyes were hazel colored. A square, jutted jaw that he'd inherited from his mother, kept him from being handsome, and in Violet's opinion, the well-trimmed mustache didn't enhance his appearance a great deal, but overall his looks were certainly worthy of notice. In height, he stood eye-level with Violet, his body slender. He was a man to be admired, and he had earned Violet's regard both because of his personality and his proficiency as an administrator.

Despite the heavy traffic, they reached the restaurant at the appointed time. They entered a room filled with celebrating guests, and Larry introduced Violet to his extended family. Larry's brother, William, was a frequent visitor in Maitland, and she already knew him and his wife.

As everyone began to eat the first course, Larry devoted his attention to his maternal aunt on his left, and Mrs. Holland chatted graciously with Violet, but eventually the conversation turned to a subject that distressed Violet. Was it by design or only accidental that Mrs. Holland asked, "Are you related to the Kansas City Conleys, Violet?"

"I don't know anyone in Kansas City."

"That's too bad, for those Conleys are prominent, both politically and socially." Mrs. Holland leaned back to let the waiter take her plate, sparing Violet the necessity to comment. She had been born in Kansas, so she could be related to the Conleys Mrs. Holland mentioned, but she didn't ask whether Mrs. Holland referred to the city in Missouri or Kansas. It wasn't wise to ask the matriarch of the Holland family too many questions.

"Where do your relatives live?" the woman persisted, and Violet decided this was Mrs. Holland's way of checking her eligibility to enter the Holland family. Larry *must* be getting serious in his attentions to her.

Choosing her words carefully, Violet said, "I know nothing about my father's family. He died when I was two years old, and I went to live with my Aunt Ruth in Minnesota. I don't know any Conleys except myself."

"And your mother?"

"I lost her about the same time, so I'm fortunate that Aunt Ruth wanted me. She gave me a good home."

"I would like to meet your Aunt Ruth sometime."

"Perhaps you can the next time she comes to Maitland. She visits two or three times each year."

Violet's hands were clammy with cold sweat, and she laid down her fork, slipped her hands under the table and wiped them on the napkin. She was trembling inside, but she hoped it wasn't obvious to Mrs. Holland. William summoned his mother to cut the birthday cake, and when they returned to the table for dessert and coffee, Mrs. Holland didn't question her again, but Violet was nervous and apprehensive the rest of the evening.

The next day, Thursday, was pure bedlam for Violet as she spent the day in the gym guiding excited students as they assembled their projects. Tables had been placed in close proximity to accommodate the two hundred exhibits. Violet was pleased with most of the students' work, relieved that she didn't have to choose the best entry. Janie's project brought tears to her eyes, and she wondered how the girl, in the face of her ostracism, had the courage to display the evidence of what her life had been as a runaway.

The exhibit, titled Life on the Street, was enclosed in a shadow box, and many of the models were three-dimensional. Although Violet knew little about art, even she could tell that the girl had great creative ability, and she decided to encourage Janie to enroll in some art courses. The background of the box was a cityscape, a dark backdrop of brick buildings, but the attached figures were in vivid colors.

The scene portrayed the outcast, the struggling poor, the homeless, as well as troubled teenagers—all victims of an existence that had lost its meaning, lost all hope and faith.

The caption at the bottom said it all. "There, except for the Grace of God, goeth I."

Violet was careful not to comment on the projects, for she didn't want to give any of the pupils false hopes when she would have no part in the decision making. All day long, as she worked to arrange the exhibits, she thought of Janie and what her life must have been as a runaway. She wanted to help the girl, but where did compassion end and meddling start?

To take her mind from Janie's problems, Violet thought of Misty Gibson's poor efforts to produce a replica of the White House. The columns sagged, and instead of being white, glue had seeped through the paint, leaving the structure a sickly gray. She and Roger had exchanged amused glances when he had carried his daughter's project into the gym. Misty was a good cheerleader, and popular with the other students, but she wasn't overburdened with artistic talent. Jason, Roger's oldest, was much like his father in personality and appearance, but Misty's blond hair and fair features indicated that she must favor her mother.

Three judges from adjoining counties met in the gym at the close of the school day to make their selections and the teachers went home. Violet resisted the urge to return in the evening to learn the judges' decision, and she was able to say honestly to the dozens of telephone calls from anxious students, "I don't have any idea whom the judges chose. We'll have to wait until tomorrow to see."

But before bedtime she did know the judges' decision, and she learned it in a revolting way that both angered and disillusioned her. When the phone rang at ten o'clock, she was pleased to hear Larry's voice. She had been so busy all day that she hadn't exchanged words with him.

After greeting her, Larry said, "I'm at the school now, and we have a problem that I think should be corrected before the students arrive tomorrow. Janie Skeen was not only awarded first place in her grade, but she was given the Best of Show award. You know what that means."

"Oh, yes, and I'm delighted. I thought her exhibit was fabulous, and it certainly deserves to be entered in the regional exhibition."

"Well, I'm not happy about it, and I want those awards changed."

Not willing to believe what she was hearing, Violet said, "Why?"

"Would you want a girl with her reputation to represent us at a regional function?"

"And why not?" Violet demanded, trying not to sound belligerent.

"It's unthinkable. There are other projects just as deserving as hers, and it's going to cause trouble with our most supportive parents if we allow Janie to be the winner. I'll admit her exhibit is realistic, and it should be—she has obviously seen all of that first-hand."

Violet felt sick. She had always admired Larry for his ability as an administrator and his fairness to the staff. Until now, she hadn't considered that Larry was influenced by his mother's narrow opinions. She conceded that many of the parents would be angry, for there had been some strenuous objection when Janie enrolled in the school. Violet had dealt with angry parents many times, but always before she had Larry's support. He obviously wouldn't support her now, but to do what he suggested was repugnant.

"Larry, I will not change those awards."

"Then, I'll do it. If you haven't seen them, you don't even know who was chosen."

"But I *will* know, for the judges send me a copy of their deliberations and the winners' names. And," she paused to draw a deep breath, "if Janie doesn't have the recognition she deserves, I'll make their report public."

"You're making a mistake," Larry said angrily and terminated the conversation.

Violet didn't even go to bed for she knew she would never sleep. She agreed with Larry that many of the parents would complain long and loud about Janie being chosen, and she had enjoyed a good rapport with the parents, who had endorsed everything she wanted to do. She didn't want to lose their support. But why should they blame her?

And what about her relationship with Larry? His attention had given Violet more self-confidence than she had ever had. She enjoyed the prestige she had gained in Maitland because she was a part of the Holland circle. More than that, their relationship seemed to be serious.

Was it necessary to sacrifice her future as a teacher, and her bond with Larry for the sake of a girl she had known such a short while? Violet had to honestly admit that the cost seemed high, but her conscience and ethical upbringing wouldn't let her do otherwise.

She could almost hear Aunt Ruth say, "Right is right and wrong is wrong. You can't ride the fence between the two. Nobody has ever said that living an upright life is easy."

She envisioned Tom Walker, the minister at the local church she attended. He had preached a sermon on integrity a few weeks ago. His theme Scripture had been from Psalm 101, "No one who practices deceit will dwell in my house; no one who speaks falsely will stand in my presence."

And there was Roger Gibson, a man she admired. More than once she had heard him say to his youth group, when he was challenging them to live a cut above the average, "It is better, if it is God's will, to suffer for doing good than for doing evil."

It was a difficult decision to make, but as a Christian, a teacher, and a friend to Janie, she couldn't give in to Larry's demands. She would have to face critical parents without his support.

A cup of strong coffee, a cinnamon roll, and a hot shower did little to bolster her courage when she set out early for school. She had to be on hand to answer students' questions or complaints if there were any. Violet went first to the gym and checked the projects. She breathed a sigh of relief when she saw that Janie's exhibit still had the Best of Show purple medallion, so she wouldn't have to confront Larry publicly on that.

Overall, she was pleased with the awards and didn't see why anyone should have any just complaints. Violet entered her room a half hour before any students were due, which gave her time to review her lesson plans. Her mind had been blank on everyday matters since Larry had called last night. After readying the equipment she would need for the day, Violet accessed the Internet. She felt faint with relief when she read her one E-mail letter: "You were right, of course, and I apologize. If there are any complaints, I'll try to field them in the office. Dinner tomorrow evening? Larry."

Feeling as giddy as a kite in a strong March wind, Violet clicked the Reply to Author button, and typed in, "Sounds great to me. I'll be ready at six."

When a bouquet of roses arrived during her prep period, Violet concluded that her friendship meant as much to Larry as his did to her.

Although no one made any complaint to her about the judges' decisions, Violet was alert to an undercurrent of discontent among the student body. As soon as the gym opened and the students learned the outcome, Janie had rushed into Violet's room.

"I can't believe I won, Miss Conley. You were right—the judges didn't know anything about me."

"It was a good project, Janie, and I'm pleased for you."

"Does this mean that I can be entered in the regional competition?"

"Yes, but it won't be until January, since all of the high schools don't have their fairs as early as we do. The regional fair is held in Springfield, Missouri, and I'll take you to it if that's all right with your guardian. It's during a weekend so we won't miss much school."

Later, when Janie entered the room for her class time, her enthusiasm had waned, and Violet detected angry glances in her direction by some students, but they did nothing for which Violet could reprimand them. No doubt, in the hallways, they were giving Janie a rough time. At the close of the day, Janie came into Violet's room, and though she was shedding no tears, her lips trembled.

"My exhibit had been pushed to the floor. It's ruined." Violet was so angry, she didn't dare speak. Disregarding the rules, she put her arms around Janie, and the girl started sobbing.

"I knew my good luck wouldn't hold. Nothing ever goes right for me."

Through clenched teeth, Violet said, "It *is* going right for you. You *will* go to that regional competition. You'll have plenty of time to redo your project. Let's go check on it."

As they started out the door, Violet saw the large form of Roger Gibson swinging down the hallway. His figure was even more prepossessing in his smart, brown uniform.

"Hi. I came to get Misty's project." He looked from Violet's angry face to Janie's tear-streaked one. "Is something wrong?"

"Janie's exhibit was awarded the Best of Show medallion, but someone pushed it on the floor. I'm going to see how badly it's damaged. I'm determined that she's going to the regional competition, if she has to do a whole new exhibit."

"Of course she is," Roger said, and he put his arm over Janie's shoulders. "Come on. I'll help you pick up the pieces and go from there." Roger's support was as welcome to Violet as Larry's had been.

Miraculously, the shadow box had only a few damaged places, which could easily be repaired. The models had all pulled loose from the box, but only one was broken. Roger knelt on the floor and helped Janie pick up the items.

"No problem at all to put your exhibit back together," Roger said. "As soon as I get Misty's project, I'll take you home so you won't have to carry this."

"Oh, no," Janie said quickly, "I thank you, but I don't want to ride home in a police cruiser. Mrs. Grady or the neighbors might think I'm in trouble." Roger's gaze met Violet's over the girl's head, and his brown eyes were compassionate.

"Very well," he said, "but I do want to invite you to our teen group at the church. You will find a welcome there."

"I'm not so sure about that. Some of the teens who attend your church aren't friendly here at school. I'll continue to worship with Mrs. Grady. Very few young people go to that church, and I'm accepted by the adults."

The matter-of-fact way the girl talked about her os-

tracism crushed Violet. So much stoicism in a girl of
that age wasn't healthy. "If you won't let Lieutenant
Gibson take you home, I'll walk with you and be sure
you don't have any more trouble. I want to see you
home safely with your project."

Janie nodded assent, and Roger moved toward
Misty's project. "I still want you to join our teen
group, Janie. Think about it." The grim expression on
his face indicated that he would have some stern words
to say to the youth he counseled. "I'll see you at
church on Sunday, Violet."

Since he had bidden her goodbye in that manner,
Violet didn't expect to hear any more from Roger until
Sunday, so it was with some surprise that she opened
her door to him, still in uniform, Friday evening.

He removed his hat. "I have something I need to
ask you, Violet. Is it all right for me to come in?"

Violet unlocked the storm door and motioned him
inside. Obviously this wasn't a social call. He twirled
his hat around in his hands a time or two, and his
demeanor puzzled Violet. She had never known Roger
to be ill at ease.

"Violet, do you know Linda Conley, an inmate in
a correctional facility in Topeka, Kansas?"

Roger's face blurred, Violet's hands fluttered nervously, and her body sank slowly toward the floor.

Chapter Two

Violet didn't black out completely, and she felt Roger's arm around her, leading her to the couch. He pressed her head forward to her knees.

"Hold on a minute." Roger's voice sounded a long way off. Soon, he sat beside her on the couch, supported her head and wiped her face with a cool, damp cloth. He brought a glass of water and forced a few drops between her lips. She had trouble breathing, and she gasped for air.

"Tell me I'm dreaming, Roger. I can't believe you said what you did."

Roger smoothed the damp hair back from her face, for he had been overzealous in wetting the cloth.

"It's true, Violet. I received a call about her a few minutes ago."

Violet caught his hand. "Tell me everything."

"Linda Conley, a life prisoner, has terminal cancer, with a life expectancy of six months. They're looking for her next of kin to give her a home so she won't have to die in prison."

Violet shuddered and shook her head in disbelief, grasping Roger's hand as if it were a lifeline. "Roger, you can't understand what you've just said to me. I've never needed a friend more than I do now."

He squeezed her hand. "You have a friend, so don't worry. Whatever it is you're facing, I'll be with you all the way."

She sat up, pressing her hand to her forehead. "Who else knows about that phone call?" she asked finally.

"No one in Maitland. Fortunately, I was alone in the office when the call came in."

"I won't lie to you, but I would rather die than answer that question. I thought when I moved to Maitland, I had left the past behind, and now it's pursued me here."

Roger patted her hand. "Your past doesn't matter to me, and I wouldn't have approached you if it wasn't my official duty. I don't want to do anything that will hurt you, but you know I can't return that call and say I couldn't find the answer. From your response, it's obvious you do know Linda Conley."

Violet smiled slightly. "One of the things I've always admired about you, Roger, is that you do what you think is right regardless of the consequences, so I would never blame you for doing your duty because it involves me. It's just difficult to unearth the past."

"Is Linda related to you?"

"Linda Conley is my mother, but I don't remember ever seeing her, because I was only two years old when she shot and killed my father."

Violet hadn't looked at Roger when she blurted out the truth. The words left a bitter nasty taste in her mouth. After a moment, she glanced sideways to see how Roger had taken the news. His brown eyes were deep dark pools of despair, also displaying another emotion. Was it shock? In his line of work, Roger often encountered appalling situations, and she thought he would be hardened to it by now, but his face registered horror. And no wonder, Violet conceded. A law officer would think twice before befriending a murderess's child. If this news circulated around Maitland, she could bid Larry goodbye, but would she lose Roger's friendship, too?

Lowering her lashes, she said softly, "Think any less of me than you did a few minutes ago? Do you still consider me a reputable teacher for your daughter?"

Roger moved closer to Violet, his arm encircled her shoulders, and he shook her gently. "Stop that kind of talk. I'll admit I'm concerned, but only for your sake. What a burden you've carried all of your life! I have wondered occasionally why you didn't talk about your family, but I thought that was your business, and it really didn't matter to me."

Violet buried her head on his shoulder, and his hands roamed soothingly over her curly hair.

"Do you want to tell me any more about it?"

"I really don't know much more than that. I've always lived with my mother's sister and her husband, and I have their version of the episode. Aunt Ruth said that my mother acted in self-defense, but that my father was from a wealthy family, and normally, a large portion of their money would have come to my mother and me, so the Conleys tried to prove that she had murdered him to justify stealing my inheritance. They had enough money to hire the most powerful lawyers. My aunt feels my mother's attorney was not capable of standing up to such high-powered lawyers. The verdict was guilty, and she was sentenced to life imprisonment without mercy.''

"Have you had any contact with your father's family?''

"None! I don't even know where they live. My Aunt Ruth wouldn't tell me anything about them. My uncle was an archaeologist, and he and Aunt Ruth traveled all over the world, but after they took me in, she stopped going with him, and moved with me to Minnesota. That's where I grew up, and after I graduated from college, Aunt Ruth thought I would be better off not to return to her home. She wanted me to be hard to find should the Conleys ever try, for she feared that if I was my father's heir, they might try to dispose of me. I thought it was a rather ridiculous idea, but she's right about most things, so I was eager to move to Illinois.''

"And you've been happy here?''

"I have never enjoyed complete happiness. I've always felt unwanted, rejected by my father's people and my mother. I can't forgive them for that, and it eats away at my peace of mind.''

"But if your mother was sent to prison when you were a child, she couldn't have done much for you. I don't consider that rejection. Didn't you ever go to see her?''

"Vaguely, I remember going to a large brick building when I was a child and seeing a woman, but Aunt Ruth said that my mother didn't want me exposed to a prison environment. She thought the experience of seeing her incarcerated would be psychologically harmful to me. She told Aunt Ruth not to contact her again.''

Violet paused. She had to rein in her emotions and

bolster her courage before she told Roger anything else. She took a deep breath and settled into one corner of the couch with her feet curled under her body.

"So not having a real, live mother, I fantasized endlessly about one. As I walked home from school, I imagined that my mother would meet me at the door with a kiss and a hug, and take me to the kitchen for fresh-baked cookies and milk. It was my mother, not Aunt Ruth, who dried my tears, and bandaged my knee when I fell off my bike. And she kissed me fondly beaming with pride when I brought home excellent report cards. She was beautiful, kind and sympathetic, and she made me happy." Violet shook her head to rid her mind of a comforting childhood dream.

"The year I graduated from college, I had occasion to be traveling through Kansas, and I found out where she was imprisoned, and feeling self-righteous and full of sweetness and light, I went to see her. She refused to see me. My own mother refused to see me!" Violet struggled for self-control, but her usual well-modulated voice gave away her emotions. "Can you imagine that?"

"But why?" Roger said compassionately. "Surely she gave a reason."

"Oh, yes, she sent back a message that she wanted me to leave and forget I had a mother, that a meeting wouldn't do either of us any good. To my dying day, I'll never forget how that hurt me." She paused and wouldn't meet Roger's eyes when she said, "And may God forgive me for such an unchristian thought, but when I wanted to see her, she told me to forget that I had a mother—now that she's dying, she wants me to take her in."

"I'm not so sure about that. The woman who tele-

phoned me said they tried to get Mrs. Conley to tell
them if she had any relatives, and she refused to name
anyone. They traced you through your birth records
and Social Security number, and when they asked your
mother if you were her daughter, she responded that
she had never heard of you."

"Still rejecting me!"

"I don't think so. I believe she's still trying to protect you."

"If she doesn't want to come to me, why are they
forcing the issue?"

"I asked that question, and I received a runaround
answer. Some kind of new regulation gives prisons the
option to parole terminally ill patients. It may be that
they don't have the staff to take care of her, but they
are going to release her, if not to the next of kin, then
to a nursing home, where she can receive proper
care."

"I don't see how I can possibly bring her here. I
have no feeling for her as a mother—it would be like
taking in a stranger. Besides the fact that it would
upset my whole life-style, how can I afford to do it?
I'm living on a shoestring budget now, and there is no
way that I can assume her medical expenses."

"Then she isn't eligible for Medicare?"

"No, I'm sure of that. I think she was only twenty
when I was born, so that will put her in her midforties.
She's still a young woman." Violet went into the bedroom and came back with a photo of a man, woman,
and baby.

"That's the only picture I have of my parents, and
I would assume I was about a year old when the picture was taken. Aunt Ruth gave that to me when I
started asking about my parents. They appear to be a

happy couple, don't they? What could have happened in a year's time to cause such a crime?''

Roger took the picture and looked at it closely. Linda Conley was a petite woman with brown hair and eyes. Her husband, Ryan, was handsome with close-cropped black wavy hair and blue eyes. White teeth gleamed below a small black mustache. His expression and posture spoke of a strong sense of determination, while his wife's expression indicated a low-key personality.

"His death may have been an accident, but if his parents were vindictive as you've heard, they might have pushed for your mother's conviction out of revenge. If she didn't put up a strong defense, a jury could have been swayed easily.''

Roger stood up and laid his hand on Violet's shoulder.

"What am I going to do?''

He smiled, and she noted again how his face creased into deep lines when he smiled. "If I were in your place, I would do exactly what you're going to do, although I don't know what that is now. But it will be the right thing—I have confidence in your decisions, Violet.'' A sudden burst of wind sent an onslaught of rain against the window, and Violet shivered. Roger sat beside her again and took her hand. "Don't try to give me an answer now. I told the woman I would return her call in a few days. I didn't even indicate that I knew anyone by the name of Conley. Take some time to think it over.''

"I'll have to. Thanks for understanding, Roger.''

He gently squeezed her hand before releasing it. "What are friends for, anyway?''

Violet doubted that she would sleep, but since she

hadn't slept the night before, she had to have some
rest. She checked the locks, turned out all the lights
and went into the bedroom. The bed did look inviting,
and she reached in the closet and removed the pretty
pink nightgown that Aunt Ruth had bought for her
birthday. As low as she felt tonight, her spirits needed
lifting, and she admitted that the pink brought out the
luster of her short, curly hair, and picked up the sheen
of her long black lashes. The color also complimented
her violet eyes. Though tonight they looked dull and
lifeless.

Violet eyes! One of the few stories Aunt Ruth had
told about her childhood was the reason for her unusual name. Her parents hadn't decided on a name for
their child, but the minute the baby had opened her
eyes and they had noticed that the color was violet,
her father had said, "We'll call her Violet. I've never
seen such a startling color."

And while most newborn's eyes soon change, Violet's never had, except to become more expressive
and intense as she had matured. So her name was the
one legacy she had gotten from her father.

Lying in bed, Violet did a lot of praying. Were there
any similar incidents in the Scriptures to guide her
decision? When Jesus was on the cross, suffering an
agonizing death for the sin of mankind, one of his last
concerns was for his mother, committing her to the
care of a beloved disciple. But Jesus had known his
mother; she had loved him and supported his ministry.
Mary was there at the foot of the cross to bring comfort when He was dying. When Violet had needed her
mother, she had been rejected. Violet's aunt had done
her best to explain that Violet's mother had only done
so out of good intentions, but Violet deeply felt the

pain of that rejection nonetheless—carried it with her always. Even if she was in prison, she could have kept in contact with her daughter Violet had always felt. No, Violet decided, there was no parallel between Jesus's care of his mother and her situation.

Scripture proverbs that Violet didn't remember that she had ever heard insinuated themselves into her mind. *Do not despise your mother when she is old.* Well, she didn't despise her mother; she didn't know her well enough to despise her. But another thought needled her conscience. *You know her well enough to harbor an unforgiving attitude toward her.*

Violet had never doubted before that she lived an exemplary life, one that was in harmony with the teachings of the Bible, but she knew that she was facing a situation that would put her Christianity to the supreme test. During her reflection, Violet kept pushing aside one of the parables of Jesus that she would have to deal with before she resolved her turmoil. Once when Jesus had been discussing the end of the present world, He had specified the criteria for those who would inherit eternal life, and He emphasized strongly that the proof of people's faith was illustrated by their treatment of others.

Violet picked up the Bible to refresh her memory; perhaps it didn't really say what she thought it did, but the words of Jesus in the book of Matthew pricked her soul like a hot knife. *I was a stranger and you did not invite me in, I needed clothes and you did not clothe me, I was sick and in prison and you did not look after me.*

"But, Lord," Violet murmured in her own defense, "I went to the prison, wanting to see her, and she wouldn't receive me. Doesn't that vindicate me? What more could I have done?''

Try as she might, Violet could not use past circumstances to influence this decision. She knew that, whether or not she took her mother, her Christian commitment was on trial. In this crisis, would she hear her Master's commendation, ''Well done, good and faithful servant''? Or would He say to her, ''Whatever you did not do for one of the least of these, you did not do for me''? Did she have a faith strong enough to sustain her in the crucible of life? She would soon find out.

Although Violet couldn't tell anyone in Maitland about her problem, she knew she did have to contact her aunt, Ruth Reed. They often chatted via phone on Saturday afternoon, so Ruth didn't think anything unusual about the call, and they visited several minutes before Violet came to the reason for the contact. In concise terms, she explained the situation.

Ruth caught her breath sharply, and was silent for a minute or more when Violet finished. ''Oh, poor Linda,'' Ruth finally said. ''After all she's been through, what a sad way to end her life.''

Violet was dumbstruck for a few moments. Since Roger's visit, she had been dwelling on how this emergency would affect *her;* she had never once considered her mother's side of the situation, but how like Aunt Ruth to think of others first. She proved that by her next words.

''Of course, you can't take her, Violet. I'll bring her to my home and care for her.''

''Now, Aunt Ruth...''

''Violet, listen to me. If you bring Linda into your

home, there's a chance that her whole past will blow up in your face. Both your mother and I have tried to shield you from the consequences of events that weren't your fault. We can't let it surface now.''

"Roger said that she told the prison officials she didn't have any relatives, and they traced me through my birth certificate. She apparently doesn't want to come here.''

"No, she wouldn't, so don't worry any more about it. I'll get in touch with the correctional facility and tell them I will assume her care.''

Violet hesitated. How tempting it was to dump the problem on Ruth. *Whatever you did not do for one of the least of these, you did not do for me.* "Please don't make any arrangements for a few days, Aunt Ruth. Honestly, it would be a relief to shove all of this on your shoulders, and I'm not even sure if I can assume the responsibility for my mother. But I'm twenty-five years old, and if I'm not mature enough now to face up to my obligations, I never will be. Give me a few days, and pray for me that I might make the right decision.''

As he often did on Saturday night, Larry took her to the country club, which featured a lavish buffet on the weekends. When he removed her coat to hang it on the rack, his hands lingered on her shoulders. "Say! You're beautiful tonight. Is that a new dress?'' She nodded as they were escorted to a reserved table. "I didn't know the teachers at our school received a raise in salary,'' he joked.

She laughed, and for a moment, cheered by his admiration, forgot the calamity about to break over her head. "I'm a careful shopper,'' she answered.

After he seated her, he took a small box from his pocket, opened it and removed a thin silver chain. "Allow me," he said, and he bent toward her, fastened the necklace around her throat and left his arm on her shoulders. Touched, Violet lifted her hand to feel the smooth circlet around her neck.

"It's beautiful. Thank you," she said, "but what's the occasion?"

"I wanted to make amends for my harsh words a few days ago. I was so intent on heading off a potential crisis among our pupils and parents that I didn't consider the right and wrong of what I asked you to do. I shouldn't have put you in such a position."

She covered his hand resting on her shoulder with her fingers. "Don't speak of it again. Have you had any repercussions over Janie's selection?"

"Oh, a few murmurings from some of the students, but so far, no parent has contacted me."

"But you may have telephone calls on Monday."

"Quite possibly, but we won't let that ruin our evening together. Shall we go to the buffet? It isn't crowded now."

At the buffet Violet asked for a small portion of roast beef, which she surrounded with several vegetables. The salad bar was always tempting, but she chose only a bowl of marinated vegetables. She had little appetite, but to keep Larry from asking unwanted questions, she forced herself to eat. They lingered over their dessert and coffee.

As they drove back to her home, Larry said, "Do you have any plans for Thanksgiving weekend? I'm flying to Colorado with several of my friends for skiing. I would like for you to go as my guest."

Violet's spirits plummeted. For much of the evening, she had forgotten about her mother. "That sounds great, but I'm not sure I can go. I may have company that weekend. Aunt Ruth often comes here on Thanksgiving, and I go to her home for the Christmas holidays. May I let you know in a few days?"

"Sure, but we need to make reservations by the end of the week."

When Larry kissed her good-night, his caress was more passionate than it had ever been, suggesting a new level in their relationship. He had never kissed her so ardently, he'd never asked her to accompany him on a trip before, nor had he bought her any jewelry. Should she jeopardize a possible marriage with the catch of Maitland by taking in her mother? On the other hand, should she tell Larry the truth about her past?

Violet changed into casual clothing after the Sunday worship service, and was about to prepare her lunch when the phone rang. It was Roger, wanting to know how she felt.

"All right, I suppose, but I'm no nearer a decision than when you brought me the news."

"You looked a little down."

"Gee, thanks—I needed that encouragement," Violet replied with a laugh.

He laughed then, too. "I didn't mean it that way. You were beautiful as always, but you seemed distressed. And with reason, too," he added. "What are your plans for this afternoon?"

"Nothing special." *Except throwing a pity party for myself, I suppose,* she thought. "You can either feel flattered or annoyed, Roger, I don't let my guard down with anyone except you. Most people think I never have a care in the world.''

"The kids have gone to a concert this afternoon, and I'm going out to my farm to exercise the dogs. Come with me. I'll throw some sandwiches in a backpack, and we can eat out in the open. The temperatures are supposed to be warm this afternoon.''

"I warn you I'm feeling rather grumpy.''

"You're not the first grumpy female I've encountered.''

She smiled, and her voice softened. "You've talked me into it. I'll contribute apples and cookies to the picnic. What time?''

"Pick you up in a half hour. Wear walking shoes and a jacket.''

As Violet hurriedly washed two yellow apples and placed some cookies in a plastic bag she felt her mood lightened. It would be relaxing to spend the afternoon with Roger; he accepted her as she was.

Roger's fifty-acre farm was located ten miles from town. There were a few outbuildings and a small house, which he utilized as a retreat when he wanted to escape the pressure of his work. Most of the farmland was tillable, and he rented this to a neighbor to raise corn. Ten acres of the property was rugged, covered with deciduous and evergreen trees. He bypassed the buildings and drove on a private road along a large creek until he reached the base of the hill.

"Do you come out here often?'' Violet asked.

"Not as often as I want to. I try to bring the dogs for a run at least once a week, and spend a few hours at the house. I'll give you a tour of that before we go back to town.''

His dogs were housed in a wooden structure in the

back of his pickup. He opened the doors, and two beagles with smooth white coats, black-and-tan patches, and long, droopy ears, vaulted out of the box and into the underbrush beside the truck. They nosed around in the grass for a few minutes, and then with a yelp, the largest dog took off through the woodland, with his companion right behind him.

"Should we follow them?"

"Not unless you're feeling overly energetic. They'll cover lots of miles this afternoon. They go where they want to, and when I want to leave, I whistle them in."

"And they always come?"

"Well, not always, but let's hope they do today. I have to go on duty tonight at eight o'clock, so I can't spend much time looking for dogs. But they'll be all right unless they pick up a deer's scent. They're not supposed to chase anything except rabbits, but I don't have time to train them as they should be."

He reached in the truck for a bright orange pack, in which he stored Violet's apples and cookies, and strapped it over his back. Pointing upward through the trees, he said, "This is a one-hiker trail. Do you want to go first?"

"I'll follow since I don't know where we're going."

He adjusted the straps on the backpack. "Call out, if you want to rest."

Sunlight heated Violet's back as it filtered through leafless trees. The forest floor was carpeted with colorful foliage, and in moist places, green ferns decorated the earth as if placed there by a landscape designer. Violet noticed many different kinds of birds flitting among the trees: noisy chickadees bobbing their black heads and saucily scolding the intruders;

brilliant, squawking blue jays already gathered into colonies for the winter and not yet accustomed to close communion; cardinals swooping back and forth among the undergrowth, picking berries from wild holly bushes; and woodpeckers hopping up and down tree trunks looked for insects.

Violet admired the fleecy clouds that punctuated the vivid blue sky and breathed deeply of the fresh air. In the distance, the two dogs barked in excitement, and as the sounds shifted often, she assumed they were hot on the trail of some prey.

At first the climb was gradual, but when they came to a steep incline, Roger stopped and waited for her to catch up.

"We've only a short distance to go, but this last five minutes takes some wind. We need to stop and do some deep breathing."

"What an invigorating walk! Why haven't you asked me to hike with you before?" she asked in mock severity.

"When I come out here, I want to be alone, excepting present company," he added with a grin. "I like people, as you know, but sometimes I need privacy. As to why I haven't brought you, I hadn't thought of it for one thing, but I decided you needed to be with me today. Even if you don't want to talk about your problem, I'm the only one who knows and understands about it. So talk or not, be assured that I'm here for you, whatever your need."

She reached out her hand, and he took it in a strong grasp. "Thanks."

"Ready to go on?" he asked. At her nod, he released her hand. "Good. I'm hungry. The sooner we reach the peak the better."

Violet was gasping for breath when they reached the top of the rocky and arid hill, bare of vegetation except for a few windblown pines.

"Our picnic table," Roger said, pointing to a level stone outcropping under one of the trees.

Violet dropped down on the rock with relief and loosened the top of her hooded sweat jacket. "Whew! I didn't know I had a heart until it started thumping. My blood is really flowing now."

"That's good for you," Roger said as he unzipped the backpack and spread it open to reveal the contents. "You're in for a treat—Gibson's turkey sandwiches," he said, "but let's have a word of prayer first."

He reached for Violet's hand, and held it in his large warm one. "God, we are thankful for the beauty of Your earth. I never feel as close to You as I do when I'm in the woodlands. But Violet has a problem, God, and we believe You can bring the solution. You know the past and the future, and we are hazy on both of those points when it comes to her mother. What should she do? What can I do to help her? We are Your servants, Father, help us to recognize Your leading. Bless this food to our bodys' use and give us a good afternoon together. Amen."

Violet tightened her grip on Roger's hand, and she gazed long into his eyes before she loosened her grasp. The genuine concern he had expressed for her in his prayer touched her deeply and she was speechless in the face of his heartfelt concern.

The apples and sandwiches complemented one another, and the cool juice in plastic containers alleviated Violet's thirst, which was intense after the climb. The cookies made a fitting conclusion to the meal.

"This is a good time for a nap," Roger said, "if

you don't mind the hard rock.'' He stretched out across the rock, put his hands under his head and closed his eyes. Violet found a nearby pine tree and sat down beneath it. She intended to think about the decision she must make soon, but her mind was blank. She had always heard, ''Don't put off until tomorrow what you should do today,'' and perhaps that should apply in this situation. She couldn't stand much more emotional turmoil. A stiff breeze riffled the tops of the pines and the limbs swayed rhythmically, but the wind didn't reach their secluded, sunny spot. She closed her eyes, and may have slept a few minutes, but Roger's stirring on the rock alerted her.

''If you're ready, we'll head back toward the truck on a different trail, and I'll start calling the dogs. They're probably resting, too—I haven't heard them barking for several minutes.''

The ridge path was wider, and they walked side by side in companionable silence. Perhaps Roger sensed that Violet needed time to think through her decision and he respected that time. Roger was never a garrulous man, but he normally talked more than he had today. Occasionally, he whistled for the dogs and received an answering yelp. By the time they reached the truck, the beagles, still full of pep, were panting at their heels, tongues drooling.

Roger poured water into a pan for the dogs and gave them a small portion of dry food. After the dogs had eaten, he lifted them into the truck and fastened them in their box. ''They're just like kids who have played out in the fresh air all day. They'll sleep on the way back to town.''

When they came to the farm buildings, Roger parked beside the house. The one-story structure, an old house, was painted a light green with modern windows installed. "Come in and see my hideaway," he invited.

"This is a good retreat," Violet said. "That row of evergreens conceals the house from the highway and blocks the noise from the road."

They walked up on the front porch and Roger opened the door, then stepped back to let Violet precede him into one large room that swept the entire length of the house. On the western side was a kitchen area with modern cabinets and appliances, a small dining area, and a broad window providing a view of the hills. The rest of the room was paneled in light oak. A brightly colored oval rug lay in front of a large fireplace with comfortable chairs grouped around it. A plaid-upholstered couch stood beneath the window, a bookcase filled with books and magazines nearby.

"This is wonderful," Violet said. "No wonder you like to come here."

"The house was in bad condition when I bought the place, but I tore down the shed on the rear of the building, installed new windows and siding, and removed some partitions to make this one big room." He motioned toward the back of the house. "There's a small bedroom and bath in that area."

"It's definitely a man's house," she said. "Do your children like it?"

"Right now, they're more interested in town life. I've brought them out a few times, but they aren't very enthusiastic. I thought Jason might enjoy working on the farm, but he hasn't shown much interest." He indicated the fireplace where several logs awaited a match. "We can have a fire if you want to stay awhile. It's cool in here."

"I have no plans for the afternoon, just so I'm back to Maitland in time for church."

"While I start a fire, see what you can rustle up for a snack from the refrigerator and cabinets."

The smell of wood smoke wafted through the house while Violet looked in the cabinets. "What about cheese and crackers?" she called. "And there are soft drinks. Or do you prefer a hot beverage?"

"Heat some water for tea, please."

Roger pulled two of the chairs close to the fire and placed a small table between them. By that time, Violet had sliced the cheese and had the water boiling. He rummaged in the cabinets until he found a plastic tray, placed the cheese and crackers and the two cups of tea on it, and carried their snack to the living area.

Violet sighed as she sank into one of the lounge chairs. She took off her shoes and leaned back. Roger removed his jacket before he sat down. "It will get hot in here before long."

As they munched on the cheese and crackers, Violet observed the sparsely furnished room more closely, and she said, "No television?"

"Nor a telephone, either. I do have a small radio in the bedroom."

On the mantel was a family picture—a man, woman and two small children. Violet hadn't seen a picture of Roger's wife, but she could see many of Misty's features in the woman.

"Roger, why haven't you remarried?"

"Are you proposing to me?" A mischievous twinkle sparkled in his deep eyes.

"Of course not," she said. "I noticed the picture and that made me curious."

"Why do you wonder?"

"Well, you're such good company. I have the feeling you've been alone for a long time."

"Ten years," he said musingly.

"Don't you miss sharing your life with someone? Raising two children alone couldn't have been easy," she added.

"At first, the pain was too deep to even consider another marriage, and I didn't want to saddle my kids with a stepmother as young as they were. My mother lived with us until a year ago, so the children had plenty of supervision while I was at work. When Misty turned fifteen, Mother went to live with my sister in Arizona to get away from the cold, damp winters here. The idea of remarrying isn't distasteful to me. Now that the kids are involved with all kinds of interests and activities that don't include their Dad, I have been thinking about it."

Violet nodded approvingly. She had seen firsthand that Roger was a good, supportive father, and he would make a caring husband.

"Now, it's my turn to ask questions. Are you going to marry Larry Holland?"

His question startled her, but she smiled slightly. "He hasn't asked me."

"Maybe Olivia Holland hasn't given her okay yet."

"Now, Roger! Larry is a nice guy—he can't help what his mother does."

"I know that. So if he does ask, will you marry him?"

"I've often asked myself the same question. I'd be foolish to say no, wouldn't I?"

"Probably so. He's a good catch, or so I'm told."

Roger continued to gaze at her, his expression relaxed, yet his gaze was somehow intense. Violet looked away. She stared into the flames, sipping on the tea until it cooled. Right now she had to make a decision more pressing than marriage.

Roger stood, stoked the fire, and took the empty cup

from her hand. He carried the utensils to the kitchen, and Violet heard him washing the items and replacing them in the cabinets. When he returned to his chair, Violet said, "I'm going to take her."

He reached across the table and took her hand. "Are you happy with that decision?"

"No, not exactly happy, but maybe relieved. As a Christian, I know it's the right choice. I can't get the words of Jesus out of my mind, *I was sick and in prison and you came to me.* Aunt Ruth advises against it, saying she will care for my mother at her home. But in all good conscience, I can't allow that. I'll have to take her and manage the best as I can."

"I'll help every way I can."

"Do you think we can keep her past a secret?"

"A lot of legal red tape will be required to transfer a paroled prisoner from one state to another, and the incident is bound to be caught by the news media. It will be better if you don't try to hide her past. It will be a worse scandal if you conceal her background and the news leaks out gradually."

"I'll probably lose all of my friends."

"Anyone who deserts you because of a tragedy like this that happened when you were a child isn't worth having for a friend."

"I've been thinking all afternoon that I probably should go talk to Pastor Tom about this."

"A good idea. If you have your church family behind you, half the battle is won. Do you want me to go with you to see him?"

"Yes, please."

"Then let's close up here and go now. He should be in the church office this afternoon."

Chapter Three

Tom Walker was a small man with a neat figure, a kindly face, and a deep voice. His hazel eyes were bright and clear. Now in his sixties, his reddish brown hair, fringed in gray, was steadily receding from his forehead. Tom's wife had died, childless, several years ago, so Tom's whole life was tied up in the ministry of First Community Church, which he had shepherded for ten years.

He looked up with a twinkle in his eyes when Violet and Roger entered. "Have you two come for premarital counseling?"

Violet was encouraged that he started the session on a light note, for she was able to smile and said, "Why ruin a perfect relationship by marrying your best friend?" Roger said nothing, but when Violet glanced in his direction, she was astounded to note that his face had flushed slightly.

Pastor Tom laughed. "I thought you might be following the trend today. I've had two couples already this afternoon. But sit down, anyway. What's on your mind?''

The pastor's office was equipped with roomy, padded chairs grouped around his desk. Tom was a patient man, never pushing his visitors to speak until they were ready, and the three of them sat in silence for a few minutes.

"I don't know any easy way to say this," Violet began, "but my mother, Linda Conley, is serving a life sentence for murder in a correctional facility in Kansas. She's a terminal cancer patient, and Roger received a message two days ago that they want to parole her to the next of kin. That happens to be me.'' The silence in the room was intense, broken only by the faint ticking of a small clock on the pastor's desk. Once she had made the initial disclosure, Violet hurried on to reveal the whole story, ending with, "I know it's something I have to do, but how can I cope with this disruption in my life? I wish I could say I was doing it out of love for my mother, but I don't love her. I don't even know her. It will be like taking a complete stranger into my home.''

"The first step toward coping is prayer.''

"I have been praying, and I'm sure Roger has also, otherwise, I couldn't have come this far.''

"You seem to have the situation under control," the pastor said. "How can I help you?''

"Although I don't know how I can possibly care for a very ill woman and teach school also, I'm concerned about local people finding out about my past, as well. I rather flatter myself that I have a good reputation in the community, and I don't know how I can bear to have everyone know that my mother is in prison for killing my father." Violet covered her face with her hands. "Just saying the words brings so much anguish that I want to crawl in a hole and die. What will it be like when those words are on the lips of everyone in Maitland?"

Roger placed his hand on Violet's trembling shoulder. "Perhaps we should mention, Pastor, that Mrs. Conley doesn't want to be released from prison. She wouldn't tell the authorities that she had any relatives. It's my understanding that right from the first, she has tried to protect Violet's name. I have doubts that she will willingly come here."

"Then I'd suggest, Roger, that you find out the particulars of her release and the extent of the obligations Violet will have to assume. If you do bring Mrs. Conley to Maitland, I can break the news to the church family, and I think most of them will support you. I can't answer for the rest of the community." He left his chair and went to a bookshelf behind him. "Have either of you read this bestselling book by Richard Cameron?"

"I don't recognize the name," Violet said, and Roger shook his head.

"*What's Your Prison?* is apparently the author's first book. His premise is that all of us are imprisoned by something, and he gives spiritual evidence that we can be freed by the Spirit. Your mother has a physical prison, but Cameron contends that other kinds of imprisonment can be just as confining and self-destructive. He refers to situations that imprison the spirit—passions, fear, jealousy, ambition, the inability to forgive, hatred, and many others—and though humankind can be pardoned legally for its sins against humanity, only God can free a person from spiritual and moral bondage. Cameron bases his premise on the words of Jesus, 'So if the Son sets you free, you will be free indeed.' I was so impressed by his writings that I contacted the publisher to see if we could invite the author for a series of lectures on the subject, but it seems Mr. Cameron is a recluse and will not make public appearances.''

Roger took the book and leafed through it before he handed it to Violet. ''I've never put it into those words,'' he said, ''but I agree with the author. I've always thought that we make our own prisons.''

''It might be encouraging to you to read this book, Violet,'' Pastor Tom said, ''because the task you're assuming will not be an easy one. You will have your own prison.''

''Thank you,'' Violet said, and she tucked the book in her pocket. Despite Pastor Tom's praise, she doubted that *any* book could hold the answers to her dilemma.

As they left the church, Larry drove by in his sleek silver sedan, but if he saw them, he made no indication. With a wry smile, Roger said, ''Suppose he will make the same assumption that Pastor Tom did when we arrived at his office?''

''Oh, the pastor was just joking.'' Roger opened the truck door and assisted her into the high seat. ''What do you think of the pastor's suggestion that you make some official inquiries?''

''I'll start on it the first thing in the morning. I should have some news by the time you're home from work tomorrow.''

As they drove the short distance toward her home, Violet said, ''That will make the day long for me, but if you call me at school, I won't be able to concentrate on my teaching."

When she telephoned Ruth of her decision, her aunt immediately said, "If you do bring her to your home, I'm coming to help you. You can't afford to quit work, and I can take a leave from my part-time job." Although she hated for Ruth to make the sacrifice, Violet didn't know how she could possibly manage alone, and she agreed to accept her aunt's help.

Larry telephoned soon after Violet returned from evening worship service, and after he had chatted briefly, he said, "I saw you with Roger Gibson again this afternoon."

"Yes, he invited me to go out to his farm, and we hiked in the woodlands. We needed to stop at the church afterward to speak to Pastor Tom."

"Perhaps I shouldn't ask, but what is your relationship with Gibson?"

Larry had not yet made any commitment that would give him the right to regulate her friendships, and the domineering tone his voice took on as he asked his question certainly annoyed her, but she answered calmly. "Roger is a good friend. I see him often at church, and since I've taught both of his children, we've had a satisfactory teacher-parent relationship."

"I don't like to make a point of it, but we've dated steadily for almost a year. I haven't seen anyone else during that time, and I assumed that you hadn't, but the past few days, Lieutenant Gibson has enjoyed more of your company than I have."

If the time came when she had to choose between Roger's friendship and Larry's companionship, what would she do?

"I'm sorry to disturb you, Larry. The past few days, Roger and I have had a mutual problem, which required our meeting, but I can't reveal any more than that at this time. You'll just have to trust me."

"Very well," Larry answered tersely. "Have you decided about going on the skiing trip? We're leaving the day before Thanksgiving and will be back by Tuesday when school resumes."

Violet hesitated. Since she didn't know when or if her mother would be coming, she couldn't commit herself to the trip, but Thanksgiving was three weeks away, and it was quite likely that her mother would be in her home by then. "I would really enjoy going with you, but I'm fairly sure that I'll have visitors over the holiday. Perhaps you'll give me a rain check?"

Ignoring her comment, he didn't say whether he would or not, and Violet assumed he was annoyed. "You remember that I'll be gone all next week to the national principal's convention in Florida."

Violet laughed. "It's tough luck to have to go to Florida and miss all of this gloomy weather we're having, but someone has to take the dirty jobs. Have fun."

"Remember we are going down there to work, but I intend to consider it a working vacation." His good humor seemed to have resurfaced, and he said, "Goodbye. See you in a week."

The time dragged for Violet on Monday. It was always difficult to motivate her students on Mondays, especially when her own mind was elsewhere. They had been hyperactive while preparing for the fair competition, and now that it was over, and the awards given, she could hardly interest them in the new unit they were starting.

Nan and Violet had a chance to lunch together and met in Violet's room to eat the bag lunches they'd brought from home.

"Did you have any flack about the Social Studies competition?" Nan asked.

"A lot of dirty looks on Friday, both toward Janie and me, but except for the 'accident' to her project, I haven't heard anything. Have you?"

"Some comments among the teachers about 'favoritism,' but there are several teachers who don't feel about Janie as we do. She's an embarrassment to them...they feel intimidated by her past. People who have lived a trauma-free life can't understand those who haven't had it easy."

If Janie affected them that way, how would they deal with Violet's sordid background? Would that alienate her also?

"I haven't asked about the birthday party last week. How did it go?"

Remembering her unease at the dinner, Violet's eyes clouded, and she chewed slowly on her sandwich before she answered.

"I had to sit beside Mrs. Holland, and she made me quite uncomfortable prying into my antecedents. I have some family members who wouldn't pass muster under much investigation."

"Haven't we all?" Nan said with a laugh. "If she's checking into your ancestry, Larry must be getting serious."

"That's my opinion, too," Violet conceded. "And Larry has taken exception to my friendship with Roger Gibson. What do you make of that?"

"That the Holland family is no place for a person

who values freedom. Think long and hard about any alliance you make with them.''

''I can't tell you the details now, but some decisions I've made this week may remove me speedily from the list of Holland 'eligibles.'''

''So much the better for you.'' Nan crumpled her lunch bag and tossed it in the waste can. ''Larry is a good administrator because he gets to make the rules, but the traits that make him a successful principal wouldn't necessarily be welcome in a husband,'' she advised. ''See you later,'' she added as the bell rung for classes to resume.

When Violet returned home after school, she was tempted to sit by the phone, waiting for Roger's call, but tried to busy herself with other tasks. She looked around her home, wondering how she could manage with two more people in the house. Probably she would need a hospital bed for her mother, and she could dismantle the bed in the small room and put her mother there. But what about Aunt Ruth? Could she put the small bed in the living room for herself and leave her bedroom to Aunt Ruth? Any way you looked at it, her whole household would need to be rearranged.

By the time Roger telephoned, Violet was so discouraged she didn't know which way to turn, and his report on what he had learned from a representative at the prison didn't make her feel any better.

''They will release her into your custody,'' Roger said, ''with occasional visits by a parole officer, but she has a clean record as far as behavior is concerned, so they aren't worried about her conduct. You will have to go to Topeka to sign the necessary papers, and she will be transported here in an ambulance at the expense of the correctional facility. She isn't able to travel any other way. As I understand, the State of Kansas will be responsible for her medical expenses, such as the chemotherapy treatments that she's been taking each week.''

"I'll need to take school leave for a couple of days, for I don't suppose I could make the necessary arrangements over a weekend. Please get the particulars of whom I should contact at the prison, and what I should do. I'll arrive there on Thursday, and if I need additional time, I can travel home on Saturday or Sunday.''

"Do you want me to go with you, Violet?''

"I can't ask you to leave your work and your family.''

"Do you want me to go with you?'' he repeated.

With his knowledge of the rules and regulations governing prisoners, Roger would be a valuable help to her, but she thought of Larry's suspicion of Roger, or was it jealousy? But Larry was gone this week; maybe he wouldn't know. But when she was concerned about the loss of reputation if the citizens learned about her mother, what would they think if she took an overnight trip with Roger? Would that become common knowledge, too?

"I'm waiting for an answer,'' Roger said.

"You know I would be grateful for your company, but that's asking too much, especially to leave your family. Truthfully, I don't know whether I can handle it alone, but Aunt Ruth might be able to meet me there, though that's a long trip from Minnesota.''

"I have a few vacation days I must take before the end of the year, and my aunt comes and stays at the house when I have to be away,'' Roger said. "I can arrange it. I won't be going in an official capacity, of course."

"I know I shouldn't accept your offer, but it will make my load a lot easier if you're with me," she said gratefully. "We can go in my car and leave early Thursday morning. We should be in Topeka in time to make some contacts that afternoon."

"Yes, we'll travel on I-70 most of the way—it's an easy drive."

She wanted to ask Roger to meet her out of town, but if anyone wanted to gossip about them she supposed it would be less severe if they didn't act as though they were involved in clandestine activities. Once her mother was moved in, everyone in Maitland, including Larry, would know the reason that they had spent so much time together. Whatever the outcome of their journey, Violet knew that her life would never be the same again. She couldn't believe that her serene life of a month ago had suddenly plunged into such adversity.

"I'll make arrangements for two days of leave from school. I'll also telephone Pastor Tom to tell him of our plans. We'll need his prayers."

Violet reached a clammy hand to Roger as they walked into the correctional facility late Thursday afternoon. Sometime she would be able to tell him how much his support meant to her, but her throat was too tight for words now. His warm fingers curled around hers in a comforting clasp, and her feet felt lighter. Over the phone, Roger had received directions to the proper office, and they were to ask for Angie Smith who would handle the parole procedures.

As Violet approached Angie Smith kind, burnished

eyes gleamed from her chubby, compassionate face, and Violet felt the knot in her stomach ease.

"I have papers prepared for your signature, Miss Conley, and then we will have to work out the details of her parole," Angie Smith explained.

"I need to ask some questions first. What kind of cancer does my mother have? How long is she expected to live? Will I be able to care for her at home?"

"She has abdominal cancer. She was too far gone when she finally collapsed and we learned of her condition. She had radiation before surgery six months ago, and chemo since, but she hasn't responded. The doctors predict that she has a life expectancy of less than six months. With the help of a hospice, you can care for her at home, but you will need some help—she can do very little for herself. Those of us who made the decision to parole her feel sorry for your mother. She isn't pleased with us, but we thought she should be with her family. Why haven't any of you visited her?"

Stung at these words, Violet said angrily, "Because she refused to see us. I was never taken to see her as a child, and a few years ago, when I was on my own, I went to visit her when she was at another facility, and she wouldn't see me...sent word that I should forget about her. She deliberately cut herself off from her family."

"Then I beg your pardon," Angie said. "She has never been a mixer and has always seemed so lonely. In the past few years, she has spent most of her time in the computer room and has been a help to our office staff at times."

"When will she be released?" Roger asked.

"At any time convenient to you. Today, if you like.

She will be transported by ambulance, but it isn't necessary for you to travel with her.''

"Oh, not today," Violet said, and a wild look came into her eyes. "Not until I've made preparations to take care of her."

"May we visit her now?" Roger said. "I've understood she doesn't want to leave here?"

"Yes, Linda is reluctant about this move, but I think you should visit her." Compassion softened Angie's eyes as she said to Violet, "If you haven't seen your mother for a while, I must warn you of the change in her physical appearance."

"I don't remember ever seeing my mother. My only idea of what she looks like is a picture that was taken when I was a baby."

Angie wrote the cell number on a sheet of paper. "I'll write out a pass for both of you, but you'll have to go through security, and have a guard with you at all times."

Roger stood up, showed Angie his official credentials, and said, "I'll deposit my gun with you now, if it will be all right. As you see, I do have a permit to carry a weapon." He unstrapped the underarm holster that he wore and gave it to Angie, who wrote out a receipt for it.

"That would have caused a commotion if you'd started through security with that gun," she said. "I'm surprised you got this far with it."

"I made my official status known at the main gate, and they told me to register the gun when I came into this office building."

Violet also had to leave her purse behind, and both of them were frisked thoroughly. After they cleared the security check and waited on the elevator, Violet leaned against the wall for support. She wanted to break and run. Perhaps sensing Violet's despair, Roger pulled her into a firm embrace, and his hands gently massaged her neck and shoulders. He didn't say anything, but he didn't have to—knowing he was there gave her the courage she needed to eventually walk down the corridor toward her mother's cell.

The guard opened the door, motioned for them to enter, and locked the door behind them. Violet was horrified by the stark surroundings. For the first time, she felt a glimmer of compassion for her mother, who had spent twenty-three years in such an atmosphere.

Violet felt shocked as she realized the woman on the cot looked more dead than alive. She was dressed in a faded yellow garment and covered to her waist with a blanket. Her high cheekbones and wide brow which may have been delicately lovely at one time now gave her face a gaunt, hollow look. The sparse brownish gray hair was straight and stringy. The woman's eyes were closed, apparently in sleep, and Violet wanted to run away before her mother roused.

Perhaps he sensed Violet's discomfort, for Roger said softly, "Shall we awaken her?"

Violet nodded, and Roger went to the bunk. "Mrs. Conley, you have company."

The eyelids fluttered, then opened slightly to reveal faded, lusterless brown eyes. Laying an arm across her forehead, she closed her eyes again. "Who is it?"

Roger stretched out his hand to Violet and she came to stand beside him. He nodded for her to speak. Violet moistened her lips, tried to speak, but no sound came. Roger squeezed her shaky fingers.

"It's Violet, Mother." She had practiced these

words over and over in her mind, wondering what she should say when she confronted her mother at last.

A succession of tremors coursed through the body on the cot, and Roger dropped to his knees and steadied Linda with a firm hand. "How did they find you? I told them I didn't have any family," she muttered.

"It doesn't matter how they found me—I've come to make arrangements to have you moved to my home."

She shook her head. "I'm not leaving here. I won't live long enough to be worth the trouble."

Roger stood, but he kept his hand on the frail body. "Why don't you sit up and talk to Violet? We've come a long way to see you," he said gently.

Roger put his arms under her shoulders and lifted Linda to a sitting position, supporting her with a couple of pillows. She opened her eyes and favored Violet with an appraising look.

"You look exactly like your grandmother," she said, "although your eyes are a different color than hers."

"Which grandmother?"

"Your father's mother. She was an aristocratic woman, a cut above any of the other family. I never could understand why she married a Conley. Why did I, for that matter?" She shifted her eyes to Roger. "Is this your husband?"

"That's getting to be a habit." Roger murmured. Violet shook her head at him.

"No, this is Roger Gibson, a good friend, and a state police officer in Illinois where I live. He's the one who received word that they were looking for your next of kin. I'm not married," she added.

"After I've tried all of these years to shield you

from the shame of my crime, I resent it that when I'm too weak to help myself, they contacted you. Please go home, Violet, and forget about this. They can't make you take me, and it doesn't matter to me where I die. In fact, death will be a release for me. I was given a life sentence without any chance of parole. So I expected to die here sooner or later. I know you're only here because they've made you feel guilty. Well, don't be. I release you from any obligation you may think you owe me.''

Violet sat down on a stool beside the bed and took her mother's hand. The skin was dry, the fingers limber. She was amazed at the immediate affinity she felt with this woman when she touched her—a woman she no longer considered a stranger, but her mother. She had never before believed the old adage, ''Blood is thicker than water,'' but she believed it now.

''You're right, I came here out of a sense of obligation—guilt even, if you want to call it that,'' she said honestly. ''I made the decision to come here because I believe I do have a moral and filial obligation to you. But beyond that, I want you to come to my home. I want to spend time with you—and take care of you. Don't you think I have the right to my own mother's company for a few months?''

After the words were out of her mouth, Violet looked up at Roger in amazement. She couldn't believe she had said that, but she suddenly knew that she did want to give her mother a home. In spite of the problems it would incur, she didn't mind taking her mother! In fact, now she hoped to persuade her to come. Roger lifted his arm in a gesture of approval, and Violet returned her attention to Linda Conley,

whose face was flushed, her eyes closed, and tears slid
from under her tight lids.

"What do you do for a living, Violet?" she murmured.

"I'm a schoolteacher, and I own my home, or at
least, I'm making payments on it."

"The actions of your father and I were enough to
ruin your life, but it seems you triumphed in spite of
us. I suppose it was Ruth's influence. She must have
been good to you. What about her?"

"Her husband died a few years back, but they both
made me welcome in their home. Aunt Ruth is coming
to spend a few months and help with your care, so
that I can continue teaching."

The guard tapped on the door indicating that their
time was up, and Violet squeezed her mother's hand
gently before she stood up.

"We have to leave now, but I'll sign the necessary
papers today or tomorrow, and they will probably
bring you next week. We won't come to see you again
before we leave tomorrow."

Linda emitted a sigh. "I'm opposed to this. I think
it's a mistake. If they had left me to die in peace, you
would never have been saddled with this responsibility, and no one would have connected you with me.
As it is, you'll have to pay for my mistakes."

"You've already paid for your mistakes, Mrs. Conley," Roger said. "I know your daughter well, and
under the circumstances, she will suffer more if you
don't come to her home than if you do."

"Let me ask one more thing," Linda said. "Has
your father's family ever contacted you?"

"No. I don't know who they are or even where they
live. Aunt Ruth wouldn't tell me anything…said I was

better off not to know. That's why she and Uncle took
me to Minnesota to live, so the Conleys couldn't trace
me. I haven't any desire to know my paternal relatives.''

Linda nodded assent. ''In that case, I'll be glad to
come to your home.''

Violet thought she should kiss her mother, but she
couldn't bring herself to do so. She took her mother's
hand and gently squeezed it as she looked sympathetically into her eyes. She kept her eyes focused straight
ahead as they went down the corridor—she couldn't
stand to see the unfortunate individuals who occupied
this prison. Violet often thought that she had become
somewhat hard-hearted during her teaching years, but
nothing had ever stirred her emotions as much as the
sight of that pitiful woman who had given her life.

Almost in silence, they checked through security,
gathered their belongings from Angie's office, made
an appointment to see her early the next morning, and
left the building. When they were seated in the car, he
said, ''Where to?'' Violet couldn't answer him. She
had borne up well emotionally when she was with her
mother, but reality had set in. She had longed for a
mother all her life. She had a mother now, one with
only a few months to live. Somehow, that didn't seem
fair. When her tears started, she reached for a tissue,
and dabbed at her face. She turned her face and looked
out the window so Roger wouldn't see.

Immediately she felt his body close to hers, and he
pulled her into his arms, cuddling her face on his
shoulder. Sobs racked her body, and he rocked her
back and forth. Once she felt his lips on her hair, while
in abandonment, she poured out her frustrations in
tears—frustrations that had been accumulating all of

her life. Even as a child, she had seldom cried, but now the bitterness of the years washed out of her mind and soul to be replaced by a peace she had never known. The flood stopped as quickly as it had started, but Violet rested on Roger's strength for a few more moments, content to be held close. As soon as she left Roger's arms, she had a new life to start, and although she anticipated the challenge, it seemed so final to lift the cloud that had heretofore shielded her from the past.

She pulled away from Roger and looked out the window. "Don't look at me. I must look awful." She reached in her purse, took out a compact and some tissues, and looked in the mirror. With a groan, she said, "This face doesn't need a tissue, it needs major surgery."

Roger laughed and turned her face toward him. "You couldn't help being beautiful if you tried. I want to tell you how wonderful you were in there." He nodded toward the prison. "You convinced your mother that she was welcome, otherwise, she would never have agreed to leave prison."

"I really meant that I was glad to have her come, and that amazed me as much as it did her."

Roger started the engine of the car. "We need to find rooms for the night. There's a big motel a few miles down the highway."

"Let's stay there if we can, and I'll telephone Aunt Ruth as soon as we register."

When they arrived at the motel, Violet handed her credit card to Roger. "Use this for both of our rooms," she said. "I don't want you to be out any money for helping me."

"Now you're being ridiculous," he said. "I'll pay

for my own room, but I'll compromise—you can buy my dinner."

"With pleasure," Violet said, "but I was serious about paying for the room, too."

Violet's room was across the hall from the one assigned to Roger. He carried her bag into the room and snapped on the lights. "Let's take an hour to rest," he said. "This has been a stressful day, Violet, and tomorrow won't be much better. But I think you'll rest tonight."

"Yes, I'm finally at peace with my decision. I realize that I have a lot of hurdles to cross, but I know now that it's the right thing for me to do."

Violet stood on tiptoes and kissed Roger's cheek. "And thanks so much. I've been thinking all day about a proverb that speaks of 'a man who sticks closer than a brother.' Well, I've never had a brother, but you've been that kind of friend for the past week. I appreciate it more than you'll ever know."

"You don't have to thank me." Roger pulled her hair with a gentle tug. "I'm just happy I could be there for you. See you in an hour."

Chapter Four

It was ten o'clock Friday evening before Roger and Violet arrived home from Topeka, after having made arrangements to have her mother brought on Wednesday. Violet wanted to sleep late on Saturday morning, but she couldn't spare the time. She had many things to do before her mother came. She would have to make an appointment with Pastor Tom, and she certainly had to talk to Larry before the news circulated around the city. Right now, only she and Roger knew about her impending house guest, but once a few others knew, the news would travel as fast as wildfire among her acquaintances. Larry had to be told, but she didn't know whether he had returned from the conference in Florida. She decided that if she didn't hear from him tomorrow, she'd leave a message on his machine. Perhaps they could talk on Sunday, before school. She'd prefer the privacy.

As she washed up breakfast dishes, wondering how to explain the situation to him, Larry telephoned her.

"I was wondering if you had returned," she said. "Did you have a pleasant time in Florida?"

"The weather was great, but we were kept so busy we didn't have much time to loaf around. I did take time for two afternoons of golf. Our plane was late yesterday, so I didn't get home until midnight—I thought that was too late to telephone."

"I was sleeping by then."

"I'm over at the school now, checking to see what had happened while I was gone. I notice you had two days of personal leave. That's unusual for you."

"I had an emergency family problem that I had to take care of, and I really need to talk to you about it. Since you're at the school building, may I come over for a few minutes?"

"Of course."

"I'll be there in fifteen minutes."

When she entered the principal's office Larry's eyes brightened. He circled his desk and kissed her cheek.

"I've missed seeing you this week," he said.

"It's nice to be missed." He seemed a bit disappointed that she hadn't said she had missed him, too, but in truth, Violet was happy that he hadn't been in Maitland during the trying week she had just finished.

He drew her to the couch behind his desk and continued to hold her hand. "Now, what's your problem?" he said with a smile.

Violet had spent hours on the way home from Kansas debating how she could tell Larry about her mother, and she had finally decided that there was no easy way to lead up to it.

"My mother, who is serving a life sentence in a prison in Kansas, is dying with cancer. The authorities are paroling her into my care for the few months she has left. She will be brought to my home on Wednesday."

A look of shock and abhorrence swiftly spread across Larry's face, and she wished she had been more diplomatic in her revelation.

"You told me your mother was dead!"

"No, I didn't. When you asked about my parents, I chose my words very carefully, and I said, 'My father died when I was two years old, and my mother is gone, too.'"

"You certainly gave the impression that she was dead."

"It wasn't a lie—she has been gone for over twenty years. I never saw her while I growing up. Perhaps I should have told you the full story, but it's not pleasant to admit that your mother is in prison for murdering your father. Besides, I needed a job, and I didn't think anyone would hire me if they knew about my family background."

The distress on Larry's face deepened, but Violet ignored it and continued, "Until Thursday, I don't remember ever seeing my mother but one time." Briefly, Violet told him of her mother's conviction, her refusal to have any contact with her family, their move to Minnesota, the telephone message that Roger had received, and how, at first, she had been opposed to taking her mother.

"You've been disturbed that I've been seeing Roger so much lately...that's the reason. He's been helping me make decisions about how to handle this. In fact, he went with me to Topeka this week. It was helpful to have someone who had some firsthand knowledge about prisons."

She saw Larry move away from her physically and

felt him move away from her emotionally. "I wish you had talked with me before you made your plans, Violet. I know you can't help what your mother did, but to have her here will cause problems in the school, as well as the town. No one will like having a murderess living in Maitland."

Violet shuddered when he said the word, *murderess.*

"Once they see her, it will be obvious that she isn't a threat to anyone. She's so weak she can't even walk without assistance. I doubt she will live two months."

"Then she should have remained in prison and not disrupted your life. How will this affect your teaching?"

"Aunt Ruth is coming to stay with me, so that I can continue my work. We'll manage." Violet stood up. "I'll leave you to your work now," she said, motioning to the large stack of papers on his desk. "I wanted you to know this before anyone else, for I intend to have Pastor Tom mention my mother's arrival from the pulpit in the morning. The news will spread quickly then."

"I don't see why you have to be so open with your private affairs. If you didn't say anything publicly, no one need know that she has been in prison."

"I'll admit that I contemplated that option, but I doubt that we could have kept it secret. Her health records will be forwarded from the prison to the local hospital. The news media will probably have a heyday with the parole of a prisoner sentenced for life, without mercy. After I discussed it with Roger and Pastor Tom, we decided that the truth was the best path to follow."

"A principle you might have employed with me," Larry said caustically, "both as an applicant for a job here and in our social life." He might as well have said that if he had known about her cloudy past, he would never have dated her.

"I deserve that, Larry, so I won't take offense, but both my parents *were* dead to me. I couldn't remember either of them. That would have been difficult to explain on a résumé or during a job interview."

Violet was almost home before she realized that Larry hadn't mentioned a date, although for months they'd had a standing date on Saturday nights. Well, she had given him a rough jolt, and right now, he was probably trying to figure out how to tell his mother. Violet felt upset by Larry's reaction, though in her heart, she'd expected it. Instead of stopping at her home, Violet continued down the street to the church. Her heart lifted at the sight of Pastor Tom's car, in its designated parking spot. She parked and found him in the sanctuary with the custodian checking out the lighting system. When he saw Violet, he came to her immediately.

"I've been thinking about you this morning, wondering if you had returned."

"Last night, and my mother will arrive on Wednesday."

"Come into the office," he invited, and closed the door behind them. "How can I be of help?"

"Roger and I discussed many pros and cons on our drive back from Topeka, and we finally concluded that it would be well for you to make a brief statement about the situation at the end of the service tomorrow morning and tell the congregation that I need their prayers. Do you think that would be appropriate? I know that I should make the announcement, but I'm too emotional about the situation to speak about it publicly.''

''It sounds like a good plan to me, and I'll be praying to find the best words. I'll also be praying for your strength to handle this. I admire you, Violet. It took a lot of courage to make the decision you did.''

Violet nodded and looked down at her hands. It was good to know she had the support of friends like Pastor Tom, but if Larry's reaction was any indication, many others in town weren't going to be as sympathetic. In fact, she expected many to be downright hostile.

Dreading to have her personal life aired to the community, Violet entered the sanctuary apprehensively the next morning. Usually she counted Sunday morning worship with her friends as the highlight of the week, so it seemed strange to dread today's service.

First Community Church had been established twenty years ago to minister to the needs of the underprivileged in the area, but through the ministry of the congregation, the majority of the disadvantaged had become viable citizens, and life in the community had improved as the local residents had become involved in the church fellowship.

Inside the redbrick building the high ceiling was arched with heavy walnut buttresses supporting the roof, and the sanctuary had always reminded Violet of a European cathedral. The stained glass windows, dedicated in memory of deceased church members, illustrated the seven sayings of Jesus when He hung on the cross. As she sat in her customary place, Violet fixed her eyes on the window that showed Jesus looking down at his grieving mother, bearing the inscription, "He said unto his mother, 'Woman, Behold thy son!' Then saith He to the disciple, 'Behold thy mother!'"

The artist had depicted Jesus with a compassionate half smile on his face, and Violet felt blessed in the presence of that smile. No matter what malignity she might suffer in the coming weeks, she could always bask in the assurance that Jesus approved of her compassion toward her mother. During his agony on the cross dying for the sins of all mankind, He didn't forget the needs of his mother. Could Violet Conley do any less?

The choir's singing always uplifted Violet's spirit, and today's musical message particularly soothed her troubled mind. The director had chosen the anthem "I Want to Be a Friend" by an unknown author.

Day by day as we travel the road of life,
We meet many whose lives are filled with strife.
Dear Lord, in all that I do or say,
Make me a blessing, a friend, to those people, I pray.

The high sopranos sang in descant the words *Make me a blessing, O Savior, I pray* through most of the anthem, and the words filled a void in Violet's heart. "Lord, I do want to be a blessing to my mother. Show me the way," she prayed.

When Pastor Tom read the text for his sermon from Matthew 25, Violet felt sure that the choice of the anthem was by design rather than a random choice by the director. The pastor read the words that had been ringing over and over in Violet's mind for a week.

The old English of the King James Version made the words especially beautiful.

Then shall the righteous answer him, saying, Lord, when saw we thee ahungered, and fed thee? Or thirsty, and gave thee drink? When saw we thee a stranger, and took thee in? Or naked, and clothed thee? Or when saw we thee sick, or in prison, and came unto thee? And the King shall answer and say unto them, Inasmuch as ye have done it unto one of the least of these my brethren, ye have done it unto me.

The minister also referred to the book by Richard Cameron he had loaned to Violet, and which she realized was still in her coat pocket. Quoting from the book, Pastor Tom read, "Everyone lives in a prison of one kind or another, but true freedom can transcend the stone walls of any confinement, and one's spirit can soar like an eagle if the individual lays aside earthly problems to think on heavenly things."

Those words were comforting to Violet, and she decided that she must take time to read Cameron's book during the coming weeks while she was learning to deal with her mother's illness and impending death.

"In his parable Jesus showed us the way to think on heavenly things," the pastor continued. "To be involved in visiting and helping those in need can be inconvenient, costly, risky. Therefore, such service can be performed only through love…love of Christ and his children. Only through ministering to the needy can we give anything to him."

Pastor Tom's sermons were usually short and succinct, and today was no exception. He talked for about fifteen minutes, ending with, "Our individual sojourn on earth is not without a design. Our purpose is to evidence personal faith in God by responding to the needs of our neighbors and friends. God offers us numerous opportunities to become a blessing to others, and according to Jesus's words in the text scripture, only those who embrace these obligations will share eternally in God's presence.

"Often when we hear these words of Jesus, we leave the sanctuary inspired as the hymn writer said, 'to be to the helpless a helper indeed,' but unless we stumble over an opportunity, we easily forget our resolve. Before we dismiss our service this morning, I want to present a specific need to you and challenge you to meet it."

Sometimes at the end of the sermon, the congregation's interest waned as they thought of their afternoon's activities, but such was not the case today. Pastor Tom's words had caught and held their attention, and they were alert for what would follow.

"Our sister, Violet, has a great need." Violet bowed her head, for she couldn't look at those beside her. No one moved, not a cough nor a twitter was heard—a hush fell over the congregation as Pastor Tom outlined in detail, the problem that Violet had lived with all of her life and, through no fault of her own, had now been laid at her doorstep.

"Violet has not asked for your help, but she does ask for your prayers. However, this is a situation where I challenge you to put prayer into action. I want Violet to stand by me as the organist plays the postlude, and any of you who will pledge to support her during this unexpected crisis, I invite to come forward and to assure her of your support. I don't know what needs she will have, and neither does she, but it will put her mind at rest if she knows she can call on you if necessary.''

Violet was soon surrounded by her supporters, and she couldn't even remember all of those who came, but their outpouring of love overwhelmed her. She had known many other incidents when the membership had rallied around those who grieved, wept or were in want, but this was the first time she had firsthand knowledge of how it felt to be on the receiving end. She was drained emotionally as she left the church building and drove home.

In the afternoon, two delegations from the church called on her. The personal care ministry group had already organized several women, one of whom would come daily for a few hours to provide food, to help with the cleaning, laundry or any other housekeeping needs. The prayer ministry had set aside a fifteen-minute segment of their day to pray specifically for the support of Violet and her mother during the agonizing days ahead. She was given a list of six people, including Roger, who pledged instant support—she was to telephone one of them any hour of the night or day if she had an emergency.

When Violet went to bed that evening, she felt amazed and overwhelmed at the compassionate response of her fellow church members. Their support buoyed her confidence about her ability to cope with her mother in the days to come. Yet, she still dreaded tomorrow when she would be confronting her fellow workers, who might not be as understanding as those of her church family.

Aunt Ruth telephoned early the next morning, stating that she would arrive in Maitland on Tuesday.

Knowing that she would have her aunt beside her
when her mother arrived made the day easier, but still
she drove with trepidation to the school building.
Surely she didn't imagine the chilly atmosphere when
she walked into the office to punch the time clock, or
the sudden hush of conversation when she passed
small groups of students. The hallway, before she
could reach the sanctuary of her room, looked as long
as a mile. Once she had read a book titled, *The Longest
Walk,* dealing with a condemned prisoner's path to the
gallows. This morning, she understood that man's
mental and emotional disturbance. She held her back
straight, smiled and spoke as she usually did, but her
legs were wobbly, and her hands trembled by the time
she reached her classroom door and inserted the key
into the lock.

Violet placed her roll book, lesson plans and text-
book on the top of her desk. She wheeled the overhead
projector into place, checked to see that the lightbulb
was all right, and adjusted a transparency, illustrating
the structure of Congress, on the lighted top.

The door opened and Nan glided into the room. She
pulled Violet into a tight embrace. "I just heard," she
said. "I don't have time for more than a quick hug
now, but you know you can count on me."

Nan's encouragement did bolster her through a day
fraught with tension. Three students from prominent
Maitland families were withdrawn from her classes,
and she had to endure stares from her students—looks
of pity, suspicion, amusement and resentment.

At the end of the day, Nan walked with Violet to
the parking lot. "In case you wonder, the school is
pretty evenly divided in their sentiments. One group
of teachers and students think you should be asked to

resign and move your mother out of the city, but don't let that bother you, your contract is too airtight to be broken because of something your mother did.''

"But they have the power to make me so uncomfortable that I want to quit.''

"Your supporters, both students and teachers, believe that it's ridiculous to elevate this situation to such proportions, while at the same time pointing out that many of your accusers have skeletons in their own family closet. If we look far enough, there might even be a few among the Hollands. This may turn the school into a battleground,'' Nan added, obviously intrigued over the prospect.

"Oh, dear!" Violet exclaimed. "That must not happen. Why can't they just ignore my plight?"

"There's no excitement in that. You know how people are. They will ride this new hobbyhorse until something more interesting comes along, but don't be surprised if it takes a while to run its course.'' Nan looked at her keenly. "How's Mr. Holland reacting to this?"

"I haven't seen him today. But I told him everything Saturday morning before anyone else knew, so that he wouldn't receive the information secondhand.''

"I just wondered which side could depend upon his support.''

"As a good principal, he had better not choose sides.''

"As a good principal, that's true,'' Nan conceded as she climbed into her minivan, "but as a boyfriend what should he do?"

Violet had been hurt when Larry hadn't even stopped by her room or contacted her in some way, but she couldn't handle facing that now, not even with Nan.

When she arrived home from school, there was a note on the door from one of her church friends. "There's a chicken casserole and some homemade rolls on the kitchen cabinet. I got the key from your next-door neighbor. Enjoy!"

How considerate, Violet thought. When she went out on the front porch to retrieve her mail, she looked in amazement at her two rosebushes. They had been pruned and mulched for winter. It was humbling to see such evidence of Christian love in action.

"Thank you, God, for such thoughtful people."

Violet hadn't been home more than an hour when Roger telephoned. "How did you get along today?"

"Only two people said anything nasty to me personally, but Nan tells me that the students and faculty are split down the middle—those who support me and those who believe I should be run out of town. If the situation becomes volatile, you may have to come and restore order."

"I had the students' version from Misty. She told me that some of the 'snooty kids,' as she called them, had transferred out of your class."

"Yes, three of them, and I won't be surprised if there are more."

"You're the favorite topic of conversation around town, too."

Violet moaned. "I did expect some reaction, but certainly nothing like this. It's so frustrating that I feel like screaming sometimes."

"Go ahead and scream if it will make you feel better." He waited a few moments, and when she didn't take advantage of his offer, Roger added, "Do you need me for anything tonight?"

"No, thank you."

"I'll be in all evening, so telephone if necessary. Jason and I are going to watch the ball game."

Nan also called later that night to see how Violet was feeling. In spite of the support of her friends, by bedtime, Larry still hadn't contacted her, and Violet went to bed dispirited and disappointed.

Wednesday—the dreaded day started out like any other. Violet had done her best to make her mother's room bright and welcoming with fresh curtains, an afghan in soothing shades of blue and a vase of fresh flowers. Aunt Ruth had arrived early the night before, and since they didn't know what time her mother would be delivered, Violet went on to school. Her aunt would be able to manage any situation.

Ruth Reed was a stalwart fifty-year-old. Her sturdy form had developed during the years she had traveled to ancient sites with her archaeologist husband. She wore her auburn hair short and curly, and her brown eyes usually sparkled with good humor. She had an air of calm and quiet competency, and Violet felt strengthened the minute Ruth walked into the house. With Ruth's help, she would be able to cope.

When the ambulance arrived at five o'clock, a group of curious spectators gathered on the street opposite Violet's house. She wondered how Roger knew of the arrival, but his white police cruiser pulled into the curb before the ambulance driver was out of the car. A uniformed prison guard had traveled in the ambulance, so Violet realized more than ever that theirs was a wise decision to avoid secrecy. Roger and the driver carried the stretcher into the house, and a nurse followed, holding the intravenous equipment to which Linda was attached.

"How did she stand the trip?" Ruth inquired.

"With difficulty," the nurse replied. "Sometimes I wonder at the decisions of those in authority. They try to do the humanitarian thing, I know, but this woman shouldn't have been moved so far away."

Violet scanned her mother's features as they carried her into the bedroom and moved her body to the hospital bed. If possible, she looked even worse than when they had seen her a few days ago.

"I believe she will rally, however," the nurse said. "At a time like this, one should be with family. So maybe it's for the best."

Linda had been sedated for the trip, but as Violet arranged the covers on her bed over her frail body, Linda's eyes flickered open.

Violet covered her mother's hand with her own. "You're home now," she told her. Linda smiled weakly and closed her eyes.

Out in the living room, the nurse explained a large file of records and a list of medications to Ruth and Violet, adding instructions on how to submit Linda's medical bills to the Kansas authorities. "You will also have to report monthly to a local parole officer on your mother's status, but in her condition that's a mere formality. Besides, Lieutenant Gibson has guaranteed her security."

The ambulance driver brought in Linda's possessions, pitiful in their scarcity—one cardboard carton, and a small locked metal box. *Not much to show for a lifetime!* Violet put them in the closet in her mother's room. She hadn't considered that Linda wouldn't have any clothing, but naturally they wouldn't issue her prison garments when she was no longer incarcerated.

Violet felt a moment of panic when she saw the ambulance leave her driveway, and she glanced over to Roger, looking strong and in control in his uniform. Ruth must have noticed the glance for she said, with a twinkle in her eye, "I surely feel safe to be under the protection of the law." She extended her hand to Roger. "I'm Violet's aunt, Ruth Reed."

"Oh, excuse me," Violet exclaimed. "I'm not thinking too straight right now. Aunt Ruth, this is Roger Gibson, a wonderful friend. Without his help I couldn't have handled this situation."

Violet could tell that Roger and Ruth established an instant rapport. But why wouldn't they? One would have to search a long time to find any other two people who exemplified *all* the gifts of the Spirit—*love, joy, peace, patience, kindness, goodness, faithfulness, gentleness and self-control.* With the two of them supporting her, Violet felt empowered to face any crisis.

After Roger left, Ruth and Violet checked Linda, who was still fast asleep.

"Probably the best thing we can do is to let her sleep," Ruth said. "The nurse mentioned that they gave her a sedative through the IVs so she would relax during the trip. The hospice people will be here tomorrow, and they will advise us on how to minister to her."

While they ate the supper of roast beef, baked potatoes, peas and cole slaw that had been delivered ready to eat, Violet said, "I don't know how to treat her, Aunt Ruth. You know how I longed for a mother all through my childhood, but I finally put her out of my life, and it's so full now that there doesn't seem to be any room for her. I want to love her, I really do," Violet quietly insisted. "But still, I find it difficult to forgive her for neglecting me all of my life."

"Forgiveness is an important part of healing," Ruth said.

"I know that, and I want to forgive, but I don't think I have—at least I haven't forgotten my hurt." She mused on this predicament for a few minutes, and then she said, "I will need to go to the mall and buy some clothes for her, if you don't mind staying alone for a short time."

"No, I'll be fine, and, Violet, I intend to help you with these extra expenses. She's your mother, true, but she's also my sister, and I, too, have an obligation."

"I'll have to accept your help, I know," Violet said humbly, "but I don't want to—you've done enough for us already."

"I'm here because I want to be, so it isn't necessary to be apologetic. I know you want to make your mother as comfortable as possible these last days. Heaven knows, the poor woman has suffered," Ruth added, "but you can't make up for a lifetime in a few weeks."

"You don't think she will live long?"

Ruth shrugged her shoulders. "It's hard to tell, but if she's alive in two months I'll be surprised."

"I see," Violet replied quietly. As she selected clothes for her mother, Ruth's words echoed in her thoughts. Though her feelings about this reunion were confused, she had to do her best to put aside her anger. There would be no second chances to get to know her mother.

Within two days Linda had regained some strength, and they put her in a wheelchair and brought her to the dining area for the evening meal. Although her chemotherapy had been discontinued, Linda still had little appetite and she picked at her food. She did show an interest in Violet's house, however. Ruth wheeled her to the window so that she could see the small backyard where Violet's beds of perennials were mulched for the winter.

Ruth took her into the living room, and they watched television while Violet loaded the dishwasher, but sitting in a chair sapped Linda's strength, and they assisted her back to bed.

Their days soon settled into a routine. Violet slept in the single bed in the living room, while Ruth spent the night in Violet's room, so if Linda needed help, Violet wouldn't be disturbed. The hospice representative came each morning to check Linda's vital signs and give whatever assistance was needed, a nurse's aide came twice each week to bathe Linda, and in early afternoon, when the volunteer from the church was in the house, Ruth went to Violet's room for a nap. Janie Skeen came quite often to read to Linda.

Violet wanted to believe that Ruth was wrong about Linda's length of life, but in her heart, she knew that her mother would not live much longer. She didn't know how she could bridge a gulf of twenty-three years in a few weeks, but she was determined to try.

She rushed home from school each evening, not so much to relieve Ruth, but because she wanted to spend some quality time with her mother. If Linda wasn't able to come to the table, Violet personally prepared her mother's supper tray and carried it to the bedroom, and she stayed with Linda while she ate.

Since Linda seemed eager to know about Violet's childhood, they spent hours poring over photograph albums, and Linda's rare smile flashed when she saw pictures of Violet on her first bicycle, in her swimsuit at church camp, the day she turned sixteen, and the day she graduated from high school.

Once Linda said, "I didn't ruin your whole life, did I? I believe you had a happy childhood. I don't want to hear about your bad days, but tell me some of your best memories."

"There was the day Aunt Ruth brought home a white, feisty poodle, and we became best friends. Then, one year, when Uncle was home, we went to Florida for the Christmas holidays. I loved the ocean. I have no complaints about the way I was treated— they were both good to me."

When Linda became tired, and pain was evident in her face, Violet read to her until she fell asleep. One evening, as she sat quietly watching the erratic rise and fall of Linda's breathing, Violet pondered a question that had plagued her for years. *Was Linda a murderess, or had she been unjustly imprisoned?* During these quiet evenings with her mother, Violet had decided beyond any doubt that whatever the circumstances leading to Ryan Conley's death, she knew that the gentle, lovable woman who was her mother was incapable of murder.

While it was true that Violet was becoming friends with her mother, whenever Violet tried to turn the conversation to Linda's emotions or her life before imprisonment, Linda closed her eyes and pleaded fatigue. It was frustrating that Linda would not talk about her personal feelings. It was obvious that her mother was proud of the woman Violet had become, but why wouldn't she tell her so?

At school, after the first week, the tension and turmoil leveled off. No more pupils withdrew from her classes and her closest friends on the staff were friendlier than ever, as if to make up for the defection of the rest of the faculty.

Larry still continued a neutral stance. When he had occasion to speak to Violet, he was friendly enough, but he never inquired about her mother nor did she receive any messages by E-mail. After a week or two of this treatment, Violet stopped him one day when she met him in the hall. School was over for the day and very few people remained in the building.

"I expected some people to treat me as if I had the plague," she said, "but I'm surprised that you're one of them."

He flushed. "I haven't contacted you because I supposed you would be busy at night now."

"I am busy, for I think it's my duty to spell my aunt in the evening and let her go out shopping, to see a movie, or anything to get away from the house for a few hours, but I can still talk on the telephone. Or you can stop by—we don't have to go out any place."

"Fine, I'll do that," Larry said, but when four weeks passed, and he hadn't, Violet stopped expecting him to contact her. When she mentioned his behavior to Nan, she said, "His mother has pulled in his reins. You don't think that Olivia Holland will allow her son to keep company with someone having a scandalous background do you? And forgive me for saying it—that isn't my opinion, but it's the way she would react."

"I imagine you're right, but I can't help being disappointed in him. I thought he really liked me."

"No doubt he does, but he won't cross his mother. And if he did marry someone his mother didn't approve, I would surely hate to be in his wife's position. Mrs. Holland is not above revenge.''

Violet tried to prevent her feelings from affecting her teaching, but she couldn't find the joy she had formerly known in her profession. No one at school actually mistreated her, but there was a standoffishness that she had never noted before. Sometimes she wondered if this was real, or her imagination. Then when she learned that Larry was dating another woman on the staff, she was really miserable. Without Nan's company during their lunch period, she wondered if she could have lasted out the day, but Nan had a common, down-to-earth approach to life that usually kept Violet from feeling sorry for herself.

Most of the time Nan didn't mention Violet's problems, but chatted about the students, school gossip, or her own family, but the day before Thanksgiving when they had an extra long lunch period so the students could enjoy their festive turkey meal, she said, ''If you don't mind my saying so, you're really looking peaked! Aren't things going well at home?''

''Better than I expected. My mother doesn't seem to be in much pain. If the pain gets too bad, she can push a button that releases small dosages of a painkiller. Aunt Ruth says that she uses it sparingly. I'm learning a lot about my mother, and one of the things is that she has strong self-discipline. I suppose that was the reason she had the strength to reject her family—she didn't want us suffering for her problem.''

''That would take a lot of self-control,'' Nan agreed. ''When I'm in trouble, I want my husband and other family to rally around me.''

''I don't sleep very well though, wondering if she will die before the night is over, and when she does die, how I will be able to pay the funeral expenses. I'm more troubled though that she won't lower her defenses and speak of the past—her life in prison, how much it hurt her to be punished so unjustly.''

"It would be difficult to discuss," Nan said sympathetically.

"It's like having a stranger in the house. When I was a child, I longed to have a mother like the other children at school. Now that I have her at last, there's nothing to give her. We talk occasionally, but we never say anything about matters that should be important between a mother and daughter.''

"My mother is such a part of my life that I don't know how I could have dealt with a situation like yours.''

"But you grew up with a mother's love—I've never had that, and at my age, it seems difficult to attain. I know that sounds disloyal to Aunt Ruth who devoted her life to giving me a good home. But when I knew I had a *real* mother, I always wanted more.'' Violet walked around the room and looked out the window. "I think one of my problems is that I've lost my privacy which is very important to me. I've always spent lots of time alone. There was no other child at Aunt Ruth's, and I entertained myself. After I went away to college, I had my own apartment, and I've lived for a year alone in my own home. Now, besides my mother and Aunt Ruth, there's always someone else in the house when I go home at night, and while I appreciate the work they do, after a harrowing day here at school, I miss walking into the peace and quiet I've grown accustomed to. Two months ago, I thought my life was settled, but it's certainly in a shambles now.''

"I can't understand that need," Nan admitted. "I

grew up in a household of five siblings, besides my parents. The house was always filled with our friends. I wasn't married a year before my daughter was born. I've never been alone—it would scare me to death to spend a day by myself.'' The warning bell rang, and Nan said, ''Time to go.''

Pastor Tom came daily for short visits, and when Violet fretted to him about her mother's spiritual condition, he assured her, ''Linda is all right. She has a deep and abiding faith—she is looking forward to the release of death so that she can go home to be with her Lord.''

Roger came almost every night. He always looked in on Linda, and she seemed to like his visits, although she seldom responded to anyone else. Depending on his schedule, sometimes he would stay only a few minutes, on other evenings he might be there for an hour. Violet realized that he observed her closely, and his concern was evident in his eyes. Except for Nan and Roger, Violet put up a front to prove that she was coping easily with a difficult situation. Those two friends knew her too well, so she didn't try to hide her feelings from them.

Thanksgiving Day was a quiet time for Violet's household, however. She had insisted that the church women not bother with them, and Ruth prepared a small dinner that was supplemented by the pumpkin pie and cranberry salad delivered to them by one of the congregation. Since Pastor Tom was a widower without children, they asked him to share their meal, and Linda sat at the table in her wheelchair, but she ate very little.

The next day at noon, Roger came by. ''I've been

out to the farm," he said. "I've set up wood for a fire in the fireplace, and the house is nice and cozy." He handed her a set of keys. "Go out and spend the afternoon by yourself. You can read, take a walk, do whatever you want to. No one will bother you."

Why was Roger the only one whose concern could bring tears to her eyes? "How did you know?" she murmured.

He tapped his head and smiled. "Intuition."

"I'm not sure I can find the way to your farm."

"I'm not working today. I can drive you out there and then come back for you when you want to leave."

"Give me ten minutes. Aunt Ruth just made a pot of coffee. Help yourself."

She went in the bedroom where Ruth was changing Linda's bed. She explained what she wanted to do. "If you don't mind staying this afternoon, I'll spell you all day tomorrow, and you can have the day off."

"That will be fine. I can join the other after-Thanksgiving shoppers."

From her wheelchair, Linda said weakly. "You should never have brought me here. I'm too much trouble. I tried to tell you."

Violet knelt by her mother's chair and took her hand. "No one is complaining. Aunt Ruth and I wanted to bring you here. No one coerced us into taking you. We..." Violet stumbled over the unfamiliar endearment "...love you and want to take care of you. I wouldn't have it any other way."

Linda returned the pressure of Violet's hand, but she said nothing. *Oh, if only once, she would say she loves me!* Violet thought.

She was already dressed in jeans and a bulky red sweater, so she chose some heavy socks and winter boots, and put on her fleece-lined jacket. Violet entered the kitchen just as Roger finished his cup of coffee.

Violet's spirits lifted as they left the city limits and headed into the open country.

"I know you want to be alone," Roger said, "but the drive will give us a few minutes together. We never have the chance to speak privately anymore. What's on your mind, Violet?"

"I don't want to dump all my worries on your shoulders."

He patted the broad, muscular shoulder beneath his denim shirt. "Aren't they big enough?"

Violet grinned. "Well, all right, if you're fishing for a compliment, I'll admit your shoulders are impressive, but my mind is so muddled that I don't know which is the worst. For one thing I just lied to my mother. I told her I loved her, and that isn't the truth. I feel sorry for her and respect her, but...don't really think I love her."

"That isn't unusual, I'm sure. Love usually comes by shared relationships and experiences. You've known your mother only a few weeks."

"But what about a bond between mother and child that supposedly can't be severed?"

"I believe a mother's love is a unique gift from God, one that is equaled only by the love Christ has for His Church. But your situation is different. Given time, that love would grow."

"But I'm not going to have that time—she's getting weaker, less lucid, every day. I've resented her rejection of me for years. Even now, if she reached out to me, I might be able to respond, but she makes no overtures. I try to talk to her, but we never get past superficial topics like the weather, or what type of soup she'd like for lunch,'' Violet said with frustration. "I actually believe she would have been happier to have died in prison."

"But you wouldn't have been, and you know it."

Violet nodded her head in assent as Roger pulled off the highway onto his private road. "I'm also unhappy at school. No one actually mistreats me, but most people give me a 'good letting-alone.'''

"Including your principal?" he said gently.

"*Especially* my principal," she answered, "but that doesn't bother me as much as I thought it would. I've been wondering why I ever bothered with a man who exhibits such a lack of loyalty and intestinal fortitude."

Roger stopped in front of his house, stepped out and reached his hand to Violet. She slipped under the steering wheel, took his hand and jumped to the ground. "I'll light the fire and then leave you alone," he said. "What time do you want me to come back?"

"At five o'clock." He started the fire, put two more logs on and replaced the screen. "There are more logs in that box beside the fireplace, and you should replenish the wood occasionally, but I have the gas heat on, so you won't be cold even if the fire goes out. You can help yourself to anything in the kitchen." He paused with his hand on the doorknob. "Anything else?"

"No, I'll be fine. But, Roger, I feel rather guilty. This is *your* retreat—won't it spoil it for you to know I'm out here?"

His dark eyes flashed with an emotion she didn't understand before he lowered his head. He opened the door and stood for a moment looking toward the hills.

She thought he didn't intend to answer her, but he turned, and with an inscrutable countenance, he said, "If I hadn't wanted you here, I wouldn't have brought you. Make yourself at home."

"Thanks, Roger."

He waved his hand and closed the door behind him.

Violet hadn't brought a book, so she looked through the bookcase to find something. She didn't want any heavy reading, but she found an old mystery novel book, and she took it with her to the lounge chair. Roger's Bible was on the lamp stand, and she opened it first, and a small pamphlet, titled "Learning to Care," fell into her lap. The Scripture reference was from the book of Galatians: "Carry each other's burdens, and in this way you will fulfill the law of Christ."

According to the writer, "caring is a cultivated act. Basically we are selfish people, and we must *learn* to love others. If we find it difficult to respond to a person, start doing loving acts for that individual and soon love will come." He concluded with, "As God's people, we often learn to care by actions that show our compassion. One of the distinguishing marks of Christians has always been their love for one another. As members of the family of God, we must show an intense concern for the welfare of others, thus presenting to the world an image of loving fellowship."

After meditating on the words, *start doing loving acts for that individual and soon love will come,* Violet concluded that she had been fretting needlessly about not loving her mother. Right now, she was doing what was necessary. She was providing a home for Linda in her dying hours and was making her as comfortable as possible. Each day she showed her love by preparing her food, feeding her, reading to her and tucking her in at night. Perhaps as the weeks passed, the tender emotions that she coveted would come. She did hope that she would have the opportunity to ask her mother's forgiveness for the unkind thoughts which she had harbored all her life. But every time her conversation carried the least hint of the past, Linda changed the subject or closed her eyes as if she were sleeping.

Violet checked the fire to see that it was safe, changed into her heavy boots, pulled on her insulated jacket and went outside. The wooded hill where she and Roger had hiked seemed a long way off, but she decided to walk in that direction, and she set off along the farm road.

She had forgotten to bring gloves, but she borrowed a pair of Roger's that she found in the closet—much too large for her hands, but they provided the warmth she needed on such a cold day. At first, she let the wind blow freely through her hair, but when her ears began to tingle, she pulled the hood over her head.

Violet felt as if she were alone in a world of her own, except for the rabbit that bounced into her path and, with a quick look in her direction, bobbed its tail and took a flying leap into the underbrush. She heard a pheasant crow in the distance, and a covey of quail startled her when they took wing at her feet.

After walking for an hour, when Violet reentered the warmth of the house, she realized that she had forgotten her cares and worries of the morning. She heated some water and made a cup of hot chocolate, which she carried to the living area and placed on the table. She stoked the fire and added another log before she settled into Roger's big chair. In the coziness of his chair, she felt as if he had enveloped her in his strong arms and she enjoyed the comfort of his presence.

Violet didn't realize that she had gone to sleep until she felt a soft tap on her shoulder. She stretched, yawned and opened her eyes to slits. Roger stood beside her chair.

"It's five o'clock," he said.

"Oh, dear," she said, looking at the open book on her lap. She had read one page before going to sleep. "Let me run to the bathroom and splash some cold water on my face. I really feel sluggish."

He helped her stand, saying, "You looked so peaceful—I hated to awaken you."

"Oh, but I need to return. I don't want to overburden Aunt Ruth."

They hurriedly left the house and sat in Roger's truck. When Roger turned the truck toward Maitland, he said, "You look better."

"I am better. Thanks for allowing me to borrow your retreat for the afternoon." With a oblique glance at him, she added, "Did you plant the pamphlet for me to find?"

He acknowledged it with a grin, and his brown eyes sparkled.

"Well, it worked," Violet said. "I realize that I'm showing love by my actions, but at this point, I believe I'm exhibiting Christian love rather than filial love."

"That kind of love is the best anyway, because we can show it to everyone. Often filial love can be selfish."

"You provided what I needed most right now. I told you once you were comfortable to be around, but I wonder that you don't make me uncomfortable. It's unnerving for you to read me so accurately—you know what's bothering me, sometimes before I even know myself.''

He turned his eyes from the road long enough to gaze at her with piercing intensity. ''It doesn't really matter, does it?''

''No,'' she murmured. With Roger, it really didn't matter. It didn't trouble her at all that he knew her innermost thoughts and needs.

The days of December always passed rapidly, and this year was no exception. Various programs and activities at school kept the schedule topsy-turvy, and Violet tried vainly to teach the role of the federal government when her students' minds were on parties, gifts, the long holiday season and their own personal desires.

At home, Linda's illness seemed to have reached a plateau. She slept most of the time, ate little and seemed to be suffering a minimum of pain. The hospice workers indicated that Linda's condition wasn't unusual, and that she could live this way for a few months, but they cautioned against undue optimism. There was no chance that she would recover.

As Christmas approached, Violet couldn't put out of her mind that her first date with Larry had been on Christmas Eve a year ago. Since she had told him about her mother, he had never shown any personal interest in her. She had received a card from him, but it was his practice to send one to each teacher on his staff. Although she displayed her other cards throughout the house, she dropped Larry's in the trash can.

Violet thought that it might be cheerful for Linda if they made Christmas a festive occasion, so she decorated as usual. Roger and his son Jason brought a tree for her when they went to cut their own. Jason looked much like his father with the same dark features. At nineteen, he was tall and lanky, but no doubt in a few more years he would develop a build like his well-muscled parent. Jason and Violet had been on good terms when he was in her class, though he had been a lazy student, hardly measuring up to his potential. Janie came one evening after school to help decorate the tree.

The girl was losing much of her diffidence. Especially in Violet's presence, Janie reacted more like a normal teenager should, and she was turning out to be quite a chatterer. When they finished with the tree, Violet asked Janie to stay for dinner, which Ruth had prepared while they decorated. Ruth also had a knack of putting Janie at ease, so when they cleared the invitation by phone with Mrs. Grady, the three of them settled at the table. Linda rarely came to the table anymore, and she wouldn't eat at all if one of them didn't sit by her bed and feed her.

"This is going to be the best Christmas I remember," Janie said. "Mrs. Grady has decorated. She has presents under the tree and is planning a big dinner. With the allowance I receive, I've bought several presents. With the two little ones that Mrs. Grady cares for, it will be like a family—I'm eager to see them open their gifts."

Violet and Ruth exchanged a compassionate glance. Violet already knew that Janie's mother was an alcoholic, that her home life had been dreadful and only rarely did the girl mention her mother.

"Janie," Ruth said, "don't answer if you'd rather

not, but do you know anything about your father? Haven't you ever had a normal home life?''

''No, ma'am. Far as I know, my mother was married to my father, and I carry his last name, but I don't remember him at all. I think his name was Robert, but I'm not sure. There were always men in and out of our apartment, but none of them was my father.''

''Your father might want you if he knew where you were. Has there been any move to contact him?'' Violet asked.

''Not as far as I know. I wouldn't know where to start, and I'd be afraid to try to find him anyway. What if I learned who he was, and he wouldn't own me or have anything to do with me? I'd just as soon stay the way I am. I won't be hurt that way.''

Violet could certainly identify with Janie's reasoning—she knew the pain of rejection, but she persisted, ''Where were you born?''

''In Missouri, somewhere, but when I first remember, my mother and I lived in Springfield, Illinois, and there wasn't a father around after that. She goes by the name of Skeen, though—Pat Skeen.''

''Where is your mother now? How did she react when you were placed in a foster home?''

Janie dropped her head, and Ruth said, ''Forgive us, Janie. We shouldn't be prying into your personal affairs. We're just interested in helping you.''

''And you are helping me—by treating me like I'm somebody. But about my mother—I don't know where she is. I went home from school one day, and she was gone. There were other times when she would be gone for two or three days, but when a week passed, and she didn't come back, I didn't know what to do. A friend of mine, who had the same problems I did, wanted to run away, and I joined her.''

Ruth poured another glass of tea for Janie and served all of them a portion of fruitcake. Violet had lost her appetite, for hearing Janie's experience brought back her own childhood, and she silently thanked God for Aunt Ruth who had shielded her from the kind of life Janie had endured.

''Did your mother report your absence to the authorities?''

''I don't know. My friend soon got tired of living on the streets and went back home, but I wandered on my own until I nearly starved to death. I went to a shelter then, and a social worker began to counsel me. When my mother couldn't be found at our old address, and I knew nothing about my father, the state agency took over. I lived in another home for two months before I was sent to Mrs. Grady.''

Fleetingly, Violet wondered if she could adopt Janie. She loved the girl and would like to give her a home, but she wasn't sure if that was the answer. Janie should be with her own people. Surely somewhere there was a member of her family who would want her.

Christmas Day was quiet, but meaningful to those in Violet's household. They bundled Linda into her wheelchair and insisted that she share in the gift opening. Since Roger's children had gone to Arizona for a week with his mother and sister, Violet invited him to take dinner with them. When she asked Roger why he hadn't gone to Arizona, too, he said, ''The holiday season is a poor time for a state policeman to be on vacation," but she wondered if he hadn't stayed in Maitland because he thought she would need him.

Ruth and Violet had very little cooking to do, for the church women had brought cakes, cookies, and other goodies until Violet asked Pastor Tom to announce to the congregation that they needed nothing more.

Roger came early, and he helped them bring Linda into the living room. He brought presents for everyone, and even Linda showed an interest in her gifts, although she didn't have the strength to open them. Violet had never bought a gift for Roger, but after the tower of strength he had been to her in the past few months, she presented him with the biography of an outstanding evangelist whom he admired.

Roger brought a blooming plant for Linda, a popular movie video for Ruth, and a dainty ceramic colonial lady for Violet to add to her collection. And Violet was particularly touched by a gift from Janie, a tiny doll figurine of a teacher.

After the gift opening, Linda rested an hour before dinner, and they brought her to the table, but her eyes were glossy, and the extra activity obviously drained her strength. They took her back to bed before they ate dessert. Roger wheeled her chair into the bedroom and helped Violet put her in bed. Before she tucked the covers around her, Violet put her arms around Linda and said, "Merry Christmas, Mother. I love you," and thanked God that it was so; she had learned to love her mother.

A faint smile played around Linda's lips, and she squeezed Violet's hand. Weakly, she whispered, "Take care of her, Roger."

He knelt by the bed and took Linda's hand. "I intend to," he said, "so don't worry about it."

Violet missed the import of Roger's answer in her concern for her mother. She turned startled eyes toward Roger. *Was her mother dying?*

Roger shook his head and motioned Violet out of the room. "She's used up all of her strength," he whispered. "She'll be all right."

Pastor Tom came in the afternoon to pray with Linda before he went to visit several of his parishioners in the hospital. After the pastor left, Ruth said, "I'm going to take a nap, Violet. I'll be up in time to prepare some supper."

"We can eat leftovers, Aunt Ruth—there are plenty of them. You'll stay for the evening, won't you, Roger?"

"I have no intention of leaving as long as there's any of that pecan pie left," he said with a grin. Then he patted his side, "Or, at least, I won't unless my beeper goes off."

"Oh, are you on call?" Violet said, disappointed.

"Only in an extreme emergency. I worked until three o'clock this morning, so hopefully, I won't be called. Christmas Eve is the most dangerous time for accidents—people usually settle down on Christmas Day."

After Ruth went to the basement, Roger leaned back in the lounge chair, and Violet reclined on the couch. "Want to watch television?" she asked.

"Might as well," Roger said, stifling a yawn.

Violet checked the TV listings. She mentioned a classic Christmas movie to Roger that had just begun.

"That will be fine. I've watched the show so many

times with the kids that I don't have to see the beginning.''

Violet lowered the volume on the television so that Linda and Ruth wouldn't be disturbed. Then she fluffed a cushion, put it under her head, and leaned back on the couch, which was a mistake, she decided an hour later when she awakened. *Not a very flattering way to entertain a guest,* she thought, but she turned to look at Roger, and he, too, was sleeping. She raised on one elbow and looked intently at him.

Here was a new Roger! When he was awake, he was always so vibrant, energetic, and his dark eyes snapped with authority and confidence. Sleeping, the years rolled away, and he seemed as young as Jason. In fact, as he lay relaxed and peaceful, he also seemed vulnerable, and for the first time, Violet felt protective toward him. She always expected him to bail her out of difficulties; maybe it was time for their friendship to work two ways. He didn't have an easy life with sole responsibility for two children, as well as having a dangerous and demanding job.

Roger stirred and sleepily met her eyes. Lifting the chair into an upright position, he said, ''Sorry—I guess I haven't been very good company.''

''I was going to apologize to you. I just woke up myself.''

Standing and stretching, Roger glanced at the TV screen. ''We might as well forget the movie. We've missed most of it now.''

Violet turned off the television and sat up. Roger came to sit beside her. He put his arm around her shoulders, and she leaned against him. For several minutes, they glanced out the window where intermittent fluffy snowflakes danced at the mercy of a strong north wind. Hungry birds twittered at the bird feeder. Neighborhood boys walked by with shining new sleds on their shoulders heading toward the vacant lot a block away, where a two-inch layer of snow would provide a testing ground for the sleds they had gotten for Christmas.

"Reminds me of the Christmas days when I was a boy," Roger said reminiscently. "We lived on a farm about a hundred miles north of here, and it seemed that we always had snow and cold weather for Christmas then. There were usually twenty to twenty-five people at our house to celebrate the day, and after we ate a big dinner of roast pork, turkey, lots of vegetables and desserts, we boys would vacate the house and either sleigh ride or skate on the pond." He laughed quietly. "One of us would have gotten a new sled, and we couldn't wait to try it out."

"Sounds like lots of fun," Violet said, thinking of the quiet Christmases she had spent.

"I remember the year I got a pair of new skates. Dad warned us that the creek wasn't frozen hard enough for skating, but I *had* to try out those skates. I took one quick slide and crashed through the ice."

"Wasn't that dangerous?"

"Oh, the water only came to my waist, but it was *cold*. I didn't want the relatives to josh me about my accident, so I slipped in the back door and upstairs to change my clothes, hoping no one would know. But my sister noticed that I was wearing a different pair of pants, and the truth came out. Sisters!" He squeezed her shoulders. "What about you, Violet? What memories do you have of past Christmases?"

"Nothing as exciting as yours, I'm sure. Uncle was always home for Christmas, and I looked forward to that. He brought my gifts from the foreign country where he was working. That's how I started my doll collection." She got up and took two dolls from the shelves. She handed Roger a small doll, dressed in a colorful full skirt, embroidered vest, striped shawl and a white hat with a curled brim. "He brought this from Peru, the year he was working at the famed Inca site— Machu Picchu."

She wiped some dust from a heavily veiled female doll, draped from head to foot in a black, fringed garment. Only the eyes of the doll were visible. "This one is probably my favorite. He bought it in Egypt."

Violet put the dolls back on the shelf and resumed her seat beside Roger. "Your lack of parents didn't seem to affect your Christmas celebrations," he said.

"I guess not. I wasn't used to family gatherings, and I didn't know what I was missing. We always went to Christmas Eve services at the church, and one year I was in the pageant—chosen to be one of the angels announcing the birth of the Christ Child. That was exciting."

"I've always thought that I would like to be in the Holy Land on Christmas Eve," Roger said. "I'd like to walk through Manger Square and go out to Shepherd's Field."

"I didn't know you had any desire to travel," Violet said, somewhat surprised.

Roger shrugged his shoulders. "There's no need to wish for something you can't have," he said matter-of-factly. "I've had all I can do to provide for a family, and it wouldn't be much fun traveling by myself. And as for visiting the Holy Land at Christmas, I feel sure it would be a disappointment. There are such throngs of people crowding Manger Square at that time, that it would be difficult to remember what we were celebrating.''

"Perhaps you can go at another time of the year," Violet said, wishing she had the power to grant Roger's desire.

"Maybe, someday."

They heard Linda coughing, and both of them went to see about her, but she had apparently coughed in her sleep, for she lay peacefully, and they left the room without disturbing her.

"I suppose this will be my saddest Christmas," Violet said. "We know she can't live much longer."

"No, and it's well that you realize it. But I believe this Christmas will be one you will remember fondly. Although it's a strain now, you'll look back on this season as the time you had your mother and were able to sacrifice for her. Christmas is a time for joy and giving, but it's often a time of sacrifice."

"You're probably right," she said, "but I can't see that far into the future."

It was almost ten o'clock before Roger went home, and the day that Violet had dreaded had passed quickly and pleasantly. Musingly, she sat down and listened to the sound of his truck moving down the street.

"When are you two going to get married?" Ruth said.

Violet was speechless for several moments, and she stared at Ruth. "Me marry Roger, you mean? I've never thought of such a thing."

"It's time you did, then. A stranger observing you would probably deduce that you're already man and wife. I've never seen two people more suited for marriage."

"But Roger is quite a lot older than I am. Besides, he's such a good friend—I've never thought of him romantically."

"Do you actually think he does all these things for you because he's your friend?"

"But he's good to everyone. He exhibits *agape* love, the kind that Christians have for one another."

"*Agape* love is wonderful, but take it from a woman who was happily married for thirty years, nothing can compare with the special love that a man has for the one woman in his life. I don't want you to miss that, and I feel sure that Roger harbors that kind of love for you—he's shown it in a hundred ways since I've been here. Frankly, I think you take him for granted. You had better open your eyes before you lose him."

Long after Ruth went to bed, Violet mulled over the strange words she had heard from her aunt. Apparently Linda had recognized Roger's love for Violet, or she wouldn't have asked him to care for her. Why was it Ruth and Linda had noticed something that she couldn't see? Ruth's words had stung her conscience. *Had she taken Roger for granted—always taking from him and never giving?*

She wondered what it would be like to know the full force of Roger's love. She remembered that day at the farm when she had sat in his big chair and had the sensation that his arms were around her. He had embraced her a few times, but always in a brotherly manner. Had Roger been ready for months to offer her the kind of love that she had expected from Larry Holland and she had been too blind to see it? How was she going to find out?

Chapter Five

After Ruth's comments relating to Roger's love, Violet didn't feel as comfortable in his presence as she had previously, and at times he observed her quizzically as if he sensed a difference in her responsiveness to him and couldn't understand it.

Although she worried that it might be another case of "using" him, she did talk to him about Janie's needs, explaining what Janie had revealed about her parents. "Are channels available that would enable you to find out who her father is or where he might be? I think Janie is as well off if she doesn't know where her mother is. The woman apparently abandoned her."

"Maybe not. Judging from what you've told me, she could have died unidentified in some emergency room. In large cities, many incidents like that occur and are never reported to the police."

"Is there any way we could find some member of her family?"

"In this day of computerized record keeping, there

isn't much information that can be concealed. I can make inquiries, if you like, but what does Janie think about this?''

"I believe the child is happier now than she's ever been. Mrs. Grady has given her a good home, and she said that if she contacted her father and he didn't want her, it would hurt her. Maybe this isn't such a good idea and I should just tend to my own business.''

"It won't hurt for me to do a little investigating—neither the father nor Janie would need to know. What are the names of her parents?''

"Her mother's name is Pat, and Janie thinks the father's name is Robert. She said she was born in Missouri. Do what you think best. I definitely won't tell Janie anything until we return from that Social Studies Fair, which comes up in two weeks. And that's bothering me, too,'' she began, and paused as her conscience smote her. *Was she just using Roger as a sounding board?*

"Go ahead,'' Roger prompted.

"Oh, I shouldn't unload all my worries on you.''

He laughed in his warm, easy way. "And, why not? I told you my shoulders are broad. Cry on them all you want to.''

Violet searched his eyes. Was it love or friendship that she saw? She had wished more than once that Ruth had kept her observations to herself, for the ease that she had always known in Roger's presence was gone.

"With the situation like it is, I'm wondering if I should go away and leave Aunt Ruth to take care of my mother. We'll be gone four days.''

"I can't see that Linda is any worse off than she was when she came here. And since Janie's project has been entered in the regional competition, she has to go. Who else would take her if you don't?''

"No one," Violet admitted.

"Even if Linda's condition worsens, Ruth can manage. I'll stop by every day, and so will Pastor Tom."

"Of course, one of the women from the church is here daily, too. I will go, but I'll be uneasy all the time I'm gone."

A few days before they left for Springfield, Roger reported that he may have found Janie's father. He had stopped by for a cup of coffee on his break time as he usually did when he worked the evening shift.

"The man goes by the name of Clifford Skeen, although his first name is Robert, and he owns and operates a family restaurant in Jefferson City, Missouri. He's married, without children, and I assume that he was married and divorced from Janie's mother, but I haven't verified that information yet."

"He sounds like a good man," Violet observed.

"As far as I can determine. It seems that he's been searching for his daughter."

Violet's eyes brightened. "Good. I'll just back off for a while—he will eventually find her. I'll continue being Janie's friend and pray that she can be united with her father."

While Violet had often thought of adopting Janie and making a real home for the girl she knew it was better for the child to be united with her real parent.

The weather was pleasant for the drive to Springfield. Mrs. Grady had bought Janie some new clothes for the Social Studies fair and the girl's happiness and excitement distracted Violet from her concerns about leaving her Aunt Ruth and mother. Janie had never stayed in a hotel, and this only added to her excitement that had increased with each mile they traveled. As soon as they arrived in their room, which had two twin-size beds, a luxurious bathroom and a good view of the city, Violet telephoned her home.

"All is well here," Ruth said, "and we're relieved that you've arrived safely. I'll telephone Mrs. Grady and let her know that I've heard from you."

"Has Mother slept most of the day? I was sorry she was sleeping when I left and I couldn't say goodbye."

"She knew you had gone though, because when I roused her for lunch, she asked me how long you would be away. I told her it was a four-day trip, and she said a rather strange thing—'That will give me enough time.' Her comment didn't make any sense to me, but I didn't question her."

"Probably the effect of her medication. Well, I won't telephone again, for we're going to be busy, but you know where to reach me. We're in Room 806."

The regional fair was held in the hotel's ballroom, and the exhibits were to be registered the next morning, so the judges could make their decisions during the afternoon. The awards banquet would follow, and the show would be open for viewing the next day with the exhibitors on hand to talk to the viewers about their projects.

During the judging, arrangements had been made for the youths and their counselors to attend a concert featuring a nationally known band. Since no one in Springfield had any hint of Janie's background, she wasn't intimidated by anyone, and Violet encouraged the girl to mingle freely with the other contestants.

At the banquet, Janie and Violet had the misfortune to sit at the same table with a man who was obnoxious and loud. Violet thought he certainly wasn't a good role model for the students, and Violet hoped he wasn't a teacher.

Assuming the role of host for their table, the man said, "My name is Conley—Mike Conley. You may have heard of Midwest Enterprises—my family owns that."

Who hadn't heard of Midwest Enterprises? It was one of the biggest meat distributors in the Middle West. No doubt the firm was a sponsor of this fair, and no one wanted to lose that support by throwing its representative out of the room. Conley had a reddish face and a nervous tick in his jaw that spoke of dissipation. He was a rather handsome man, probably in his thirties, with blondish features. His full lips displayed a hint of petulance, but occasionally, he seemed to drop the mask of his self-importance as a Conley, and Violet decided that under other circumstances, he might have been a decent companion.

Mostly, however, Conley complained endlessly to the waitresses and made a general nuisance of himself. After they had eaten their salads and were waiting for the main course, Conley began to quiz each of his tablemates to learn their names and find out where they lived. He usually added a cutting witticism to each of their statements, and again Violet suspected that he was playing a role, that his present behavior was a facade.

Violet hesitated when he came to her, for she didn't want him to know that they shared the same surname. But if she didn't answer, he would probably create a worse scene, so she simply said, "Violet Conley. I live in Maitland, Illinois."

"Conley, eh? Not a very common name. You any relation to the Kansas Conleys?"

Violet remembered that Mrs. Holland had asked her if she was related to the Kansas City Conleys, so apparently a large number lived here. "I don't know any Conley other than myself."

"Oh, well, I wouldn't worry about it if I were you. There are good Conleys and there are bad Conleys. Even our branch has had a few rotten apples on it." Violet thought she had been dismissed, and she breathed easier, but just when she started to relax, he turned quickly and snapped a question at her.

"What's your father's name?"

"I believe it was Ryan, but I don't know for sure."

He regarded her from speculative eyes for a few seconds before he turned his gaze away.

Violet was disappointed that Janie's project wasn't chosen for one of the high awards, but she was gratified that she had at least, among 15 others students, received Honorable Mention for her exhibit. Out of four hundred projects, that was noteworthy when one considered all the odds against Janie. When she returned from receiving her certificate, Janie's beaming face indicated that she wasn't disappointed, and indeed it was an honor to be recognized in such a large group.

Janie was so excited that she couldn't go to sleep, and consequently, kept talking so that Violet couldn't sleep either, but she managed to awaken Janie the next morning, and they arrived in the exhibit area ahead of schedule. The exhibitors were expected to stay beside their projects most of the time, but they did have opportunity to mill around and see what the other students had done. It was a rather tiring day, and by midafternoon the viewers had dwindled. Violet would have liked to go home tonight, but she knew by the time the show was over at five o'clock, it would be too late to start after they dismantled Janie's project.

Contemplating these things, Violet jumped slightly when Janie nudged her. "Look. There's Lieutenant Gibson." She was amazed to see Roger moving slowly up the aisle across from theirs, obviously searching for someone. Who else but the two of them?

"Roger," she called, earning her surprised looks from those around her, but Roger heard her voice and looked in her direction. He lifted his hand and came rapidly toward them, and he looked formidable in his dark business suit, white shirt and red tie.

"What is wrong?" she asked softly when he reached her side. Roger took both her hands in his.

"Brace yourself, my dear. Your mother died early this morning, and I didn't want you to hear it by telephone. I caught the first plane I could and came to drive you home."

"But how did it happen?" Violet gasped. "Did she take a turn for the worse?"

"Ruth couldn't rouse her at all yesterday, and she died in her sleep last night. Ruth wasn't even awake, so don't you fret about not being there."

Violet shook her head in dismay. "I'll always regret not being with her. I bring her to my home so she can die with family, and then I'm gone when it happens."

"Ruth believes she willed herself to die while you were gone, so you wouldn't have to witness her death. She has always tried to spare you pain, and she continued her protection right to the end." Violet felt stunned by the news, yet Roger's words penetrated to her heart. Yes, her mother had always tried to protect her. If that wasn't evidence of a mother's love for her child, what was?

Roger turned, looked at the project and noticed Janie's ribbon.

"Well, congratulations, Janie—I see you've gotten another award."

"Only Honorable Mention, but I'm satisfied with that."

"You should be. While I was searching for you, I saw some excellent projects, so you had more competition than at Maitland." Turning to Violet again, he said, "When can you leave?"

"The show closes at five, but if I go and check out of our room now, we can leave immediately afterward. But that's going to be a long drive for you after dark, Roger. Perhaps we should stay over until tomorrow."

"I napped on the plane, and I'll be all right. Ruth is waiting until you arrive to make arrangements."

"You go ahead and check out," Janie said. "I'll be all right here. My suitcase is packed." Violet noted that very few visitors remained in the exhibit room, and she knew that Janie could get along without her. She was suddenly obsessed with the need to return to Maitland as quickly as possible.

The elevator ride up to their room on the eighth floor was crowded, and she welcomed an excuse to lean close to Roger and rest on the solidity of his physique. She fished in her purse for the door key and had it ready when they came to her room, but her hand trembled so much, she couldn't insert the key. Roger took it from her, opened the door and followed her into the room.

"It won't take long for me to pack, and Janie has kept her clothes in the suitcase."

"We aren't in that much of a hurry. Come over here." She hadn't cried, but her trembling wouldn't stop, and Roger pulled her into his arms and cuddled her in his muscular arms as if she were a child.

"I didn't have the chance to ask her forgiveness, Roger, for my past feelings toward her. I tried to, but she wouldn't permit any serious talk."

"I'm sure she didn't feel there was anything to forgive. She thought she needed to ask your forgiveness for all the grief she had caused you."

"But if she would only have talked to me!"

"She may have talked to Ruth, and if so, she will tell you now, but Linda had kept her emotions stifled for over twenty years, and I doubt she could talk to you. To my notion, she exemplified the epitome of the sacrificial love of a mother."

"You always make me feel better, Roger, and thanks for taking the time to come out here for me. I wouldn't have welcomed that long drive home, but Aunt Ruth says that I take you for granted."

He lifted her head from where she had buried it on his chest, and looked deeply into her eyes. Usually one could determine his thoughts, but today Roger's good, strong face reflected inscrutable emotions. "When I have any complaints about how you treat me, I'll let you know. You couldn't make any changes that would cause me to think more of you than I do already."

She placed a hand on his chest and leaned back to return his gaze. Almost in a whisper, she said, "Roger, what are you trying to tell me?"

"I love you," he said simply.

"What kind?"

"What do you mean?"

"I mean, what kind of love do you have for me?

The kind that one Christian has for another, or does it go deeper than that?''

''Both.'' With his hand still holding her chin, Roger pressed his lips against hers, as he answered the question with caresses that left her like putty in his arms. When her senses returned to normal, she had her arms around Roger's neck, and he was whispering terms of endearment in her ear.

''How long have you known?'' she murmured.

''For at least a year—perhaps even longer than that.''

''Why haven't you told me?''

''Well, for one thing, Larry Holland was cluttering up the landscape, but I wouldn't have let that deter me if you hadn't seemed so satisfied with the status quo. I didn't want to scare you off, as I preferred friendship to nothing.''

''We'll have to forget this happened, for I can't deal with it now. We have to get back to Maitland, and with Janie along, we'll have to continue to be 'friends.'''

''I doubt I can forget what happened, and I had no intention of speaking today, but you seemed so alone that I wanted you to know that you need never be alone again. I'll always be there for you, Violet, any time that you need me.''

They were deprived of any further intimate conversation on their trip home because of Janie's presence in the back seat, but once, when she knew that Janie was sleeping, Violet reached out her hand and placed it on the seat between them. He immediately covered her fingers with a touch that conveyed his warmth and concern.

Although they couldn't talk, some of the time Violet

forgot her mother's death, and the situation she faced
when she arrived home, marveling at Roger's decla-
ration of love, and her reaction to his embrace. How
could she have been so blind as to believe all that
existed between them was friendship? And she *had*
believed it! She had enjoyed being with him, she had
relied on his help and advice, but, in the years she had
known Roger, she had never before experienced that
tingling, breathless, giddy, awesome feeling that she
had always expected from love until he had kissed her
a few hours ago. Nor, except for a few glances that
she couldn't interpret, had he ever given any indication that he held for her a keen, humbling, urgent
yearning that had caused a strong man like him to
tremble when he took her into his arms. Considering
the depth of his longing, which he had experienced for
more than a year, she wondered how he could wait so
long to approach her. But she had long known that
Roger was self-disciplined, deliberate in his thinking,
not given to hasty judgments. So, if he said he loved
her, she had no doubt that he did.

And amazingly, she loved him. She'd never realized
it before, yet suddenly she felt no doubt of that.

The funeral was held in the sanctuary of First Community Church, well attended by the members of the
congregation. Janie and Mrs. Grady came, as did Nan
Oliver. As was customary, a floral arrangement arrived
from the school, and several of her fellow teachers
called at the funeral home the night before to offer
condolences, and to Violet's surprise, so did Larry.
While he was offering the trite words commonly spoken at a time of death, Violet met Roger's eyes across
the room. He always seemed to know her inner

thoughts, but she couldn't read his. *Was he jealous of the time she had spent with Larry or was he above such petty emotions?*

As Pastor Tom delivered his brief message, Violet was comforted to hear that he had talked often with Linda about her relationship with God and had been satisfied that she was spiritually prepared to go to Heaven. Yet Violet's thoughts dwelled once again on her mother's unhappy life—dead at forty-five, and over half of that time she had been behind bars. Before her marriage, Linda had apparently been a happy person, for Ruth had talked often about their fun-filled girlhood, so what about marriage had changed her? Would she ever learn what had brought her mother to the breaking point?

Did anyone except Ruth and herself mourn for Linda? In all honesty, Violet knew that she didn't mourn as much for her mother, as she sorrowed for the lost years that could never be reclaimed. That was a void in her life which would never be filled. Now that she had gotten accustomed to having people in the house, she would no doubt feel lonely when Ruth returned home.

She would have liked for Roger to be at her side today, but after he had declared his love for her in Springfield, he had reverted to the caring friend he had always been. Except when he was at work, since their return to Maitland, he had been in constant attendance—most of the time at a distance, but she knew he was there. Right now, she needed friendship more than anything else from him, and although a brotherly hug around her shoulders was comforting, she longed for much more.

* * *

Several of the church women had a meal prepared at Violet's home after the funeral, which Roger and Pastor Tom shared with them. Snow had started falling while they were at the cemetery, and within two hours, an inch of snow blanketed the ground. After he had eaten, Roger excused himself. "I'll need to check in at headquarters. We'll need all of our officers on duty tonight—this could be a nasty snow."

Violet walked with him to the door and waited while he shrugged into his coat. "Let me know when you want my company," he said softly.

"All the time," she replied honestly. "but I do know that you have other commitments."

He squeezed her hand, and his eyes blazed with promises of the future. "I'll try to telephone before you go to bed."

"Be careful, Roger," she called as he went toward his car, wondering if his wife had often been concerned about the dangers that Roger faced as a policeman. The times he had embraced her when he was in uniform, Violet was always aware of the safety vest he wore and the reason for it. She sighed. *Just another adjustment she would have to make if they were married.*

The house was strangely quiet after all the guests left. Violet remembered that it had been that way when Aunt Ruth's husband had died—he came from a large family, and when his sister, brothers, nieces and nephews had gone, Violet and Ruth had eyed each other in dismay, wondering how they could cope with the emptiness.

Ruth must have been thinking the same thing for she said, "We got through it the last time, we will manage now, too."

"Did she ever talk to you when I wasn't here? About the important things, I mean."

"Not often. She did thank me one day for taking such good care of you. She was proud of the woman you had become, but I assured her that I hadn't had much to do with it. You came from good stock on the maternal side, and the Conleys weren't all bad—your father just happened to be the rotten egg."

"When I was in Springfield last week, I met a Mike Conley. He was an obnoxious sort, and I figured that all Conleys were like that. He seemed rather interested in my background—could he have been a relative?"

"Possibly, for your father came from Kansas City, but I never knew any of them. But back to Linda. She wrote a letter to you one day and put it in that metal box of hers. You weren't to see it until after her death. Do you want to read it now?"

"Yes, of course."

Violet felt as if she'd had about all she could take, but she wondered if the contents of the letter might help her bring closure to this traumatic situation.

Ruth went into the bedroom and brought out the box and placed it on the dining table. She handed Violet the key that Linda had worn on the chain around her neck.

"I'm afraid to open it," Violet said, "but more afraid not to." She inserted the key and lifted the lid. On top of several other papers in the box was an envelope addressed, "Violet."

"'Daughter,'" Violet read aloud.

"I know that you have been troubled because I wouldn't speak to you about matters that were of utmost importance to you. But I could not. Years ago, I put a lock on the past and forgave your father and his family for what they did to me. I want to die in peace, and I feared I could not if I resurrected memories that would not help, but might plunge me into the hatred I once knew. I cannot go to meet my Maker with unforgiveness in my heart.

"You will need to contact William O'Brien, an attorney in Kansas City, Kansas, for he is the executor of my estate. He was my friend and lawyer during the trial, and he will answer any questions you have about the past. Let me warn that you will be better off not to know, but if you can't bury the past otherwise, William will tell you.

"On my dying bed, I ask that you forgive me, as well as your father's family, for stunting your childhood. Forget the past, and live for the future.

Your mother, Linda Conley."

When she finished reading, Violet looked up wonderingly at Ruth.

"The executor of her estate! What did she have?"

"Nothing to my knowledge. She had some inheritance from our father, but she spent all of that on the trial."

Ruth hovered over Violet as she lifted documents from the box. First, they found Linda's Last Will and Testament bequeathing her estate to Violet. With shaking hands, Violet pulled out another envelope, containing a contract between a leading publisher and Richard Cameron, a pseudonym for Violet Conley, for publishing rights to the book *What's Your Prison?*

"That's the book Pastor Tom has been quoting. Do

you suppose Linda wrote that book?'' Ruth asked. ''She was always writing verses and stories when she was a child.''

Violet rushed into the living room and brought back the book the pastor had loaned her, but which she had never had time to read. She opened the book, and on the first page read a dedication, ''To my daughter.''

She handed the book to Ruth and sorted through the other items in the box. There was a check stub for $100,000—an advance toward royalties on the book. A bank account opened in Linda's name showed that she had received a total of $150,000 thus far for the book.

''And she died without benefitting from her labor,'' Violet said.

''Oh, she benefitted from it,'' Ruth said. ''She died comfortably knowing that this inheritance would make up to you for what you had lost when she killed your father. The Conleys are wealthy people, and as your father's heir you would have gotten quite a sum. Linda did exactly what she wanted to with the proceeds from that book.''

''Isn't it wonderful? I've been ashamed of my mother all of my life, and now I have something to feel proud about. She made a difference in the world— no doubt this book has been a help to countless people.''

As Violet stared down at the book she knew the money made no difference to her. It was her mother's achievement that mattered.

''Linda was always a secretive person. Even as a child, she kept most of her thoughts to herself, but she should have told us so that we could have rejoiced with her.''

"And I've been worrying about how to pay her funeral expenses. I wish she had told me."

Violet sat up the rest of the night reading the book, and she felt as if each page were a personal message from her mother. With God's help, Linda had come to terms with her restricted life, had made a contribution to uplift others through her book, and she had died in peace without any bitterness in her soul. Violet's own faith was strengthened as she read the closing pages of the small book.

Christ can set the prisoner free. When He launched his ministry in His hometown of Nazareth, Jesus used the words of the Prophet Isaiah to announce the goal of His Kingdom: "The Spirit of the Lord is on me, because he has anointed me to preach good news to the poor. He has sent me to proclaim freedom for the prisoners." The lot of prisoners in Jesus's day was even more severe than for those in our century, and while He had compassion for those unfortunate enough to run afoul of Roman law, we have no evidence that Jesus ever scaled literal prison walls to free such captives. No, He freed those who were in bondage to sin, ill health, selfishness, loneliness.

Those of us who have broken the laws of man and God must pay the penalty. However, those who have broken God's laws have a powerful advocate in the Lord Jesus. He came to free spiritual prisoners! "Now the Lord is the Spirit, and where the Spirit of the Lord is, there is freedom." Humans who have been freed from spiritual bondage have inherited the power to surmount all prison walls. "It is for freedom that Christ has set us free. Stand firm, then, and do not let yourselves be burdened again by a yoke of slavery."

The ringing telephone awakened Violet the next morning, and groping sleepily from beneath the covers, she found the receiver and muttered, "Hello."

"Did I awaken you?" Roger said guiltily. "It's almost nine o'clock. I supposed you were awake by now."

Violet sat up in bed and pulled the covers around her shoulders. "I normally would have been, but I didn't sleep well."

"I'm sorry I didn't telephone last night, but it was too late when I went off duty. I have a few hours this afternoon, if you want Jason and me to help with rearranging the furniture."

"That will be helpful. I intend to call the hospital supply company today and have them pick up their equipment. And after you finish that, would you have time to go with me to talk with Pastor Tom?"

"Are you forcing me into marriage already?" he replied in a teasing tone.

"Then that will teach you to be careful of what you say," Violet said, leaving him in suspense.

A telephone call to William O'Brien's office later on in the morning confirmed the validity of the papers they had found among Linda's possessions. She had written the book over a long period of time, and upon William's insistence had submitted it to a publisher two years ago. She had banked all of her money, and the royalties were credited to her account twice each year. As far as O'Brien knew, Linda had never written anything else.

He assured Violet that settling the estate would be a simple matter and could be handled over the telephone and by mail, saving Violet a journey to Kansas City. Violet didn't question the lawyer about the trial that sent her mother to prison. Perhaps one day she would.

Violet made an appointment with Pastor Tom, and he was waiting for them when Roger and Violet arrived at four o'clock. She carried the documents they had found in her mother's possessions that pertained to *What's Your Prison?* and the copy he had loaned her.

She couldn't conceal the elation in her voice, when she said, "Pastor, did you know that the author of this book you have been quoting for the past several weeks wrote under a pseudonym?"

"No, I had never heard of Richard Cameron until I found this book on the bestsellers shelf at the local bookstore."

"One of the few things my mother brought with her from prison was a small metal box. I found these papers in that box last night."

She handed Roger the letter her mother had left for her and extended the contract for *What's Your Prison?* to Pastor Tom. "After you've read them, switch papers. I wanted to share this good news with my two best friends at the same time."

Roger read the letter and looked at Violet with glistening eyes. When he saw the contents of the contract, he knelt by her chair, lifted her hand and kissed it. "How wonderful for you, my dear! This has brought a happy ending to a situation that has caused you a lot of grief. You see, God is still faithful. He has vindicated the sacrifice you made to care for your mother, and has proven her selfless love for you.''

''Yes, I have such a sense of relief. I have a mother that I can be proud of—one who triumphed over tremendous odds and in doing so, brought help to other troubled souls. It's a satisfying end to a much-troubled life.''

''But I believe Linda had found her peace,'' Pastor Tom said. ''It's obvious from the words of this letter. And I've read the book several times—writing that book served as a catharsis for her wounded spirit.''

''I spoke with her attorney this morning, and he said that she had been writing the book over a period of several years, and only at his insistence did she submit it for publication.''

''With your permission, Violet,'' Pastor Tom said, ''I would like to contact the local paper and ask them to insert a feature about this book. I am aware that many people in town have shunned you after they found out that your mother was a convict. It might change their views if they learn that Linda was the author of this acclaimed book.''

''It doesn't matter about me. At first I was very distressed to be mistreated by my peers, but I've gotten over it. I would like to honor my mother's name, however.'' Knowing that any decision she made from now would involve Roger, she said to him, ''What do you think about the pastor's suggestion?''

He was sitting on the floor at her feet, still holding her hand, and Violet wondered if the pastor had noted the change in their relationship. ''Why don't you think about it for a while? She's waited two years for recognition—why not a few more days? Also, you should consider how Linda would feel about the publicity. She was a very private person."

"Yes, I realize that publishing this information would be for *me*. She's in a place where nothing will ever distress her again."

When Roger stopped the truck in front of her home, he said, "When can I see you? We need to talk."

"Tomorrow night? I go back to school on Monday, and I'll be working late each night trying to make up for the week I've been gone."

"I'm on night patrol next week, too. Tomorrow will be fine. Any choice of where we'll go?"

Violet gazed steadily into his eyes, hoping to convey her deep love for him. "As long as I'm with you, I don't care where we are. I love you."

His hand tightened on her shoulder. "The next time you say that, don't do it on Main Street in broad daylight."

"I would prefer more privacy myself."

"How about going to the farm for steaks? I have a gas grill on the back porch."

"Sounds good. I'll bring dessert."

All the next day, Violet thought about the coming evening with Roger, considering the pending change in their relationship. She would miss his friendship, but she trembled at the hint of how much more she would be gaining.

It was a beautiful evening to be out in the country and Violet felt the relaxing effects of the setting and Roger's company. They had ignored any serious talk while they prepared the meal, ate it and tidied up the kitchen. They pushed the two lounge chairs close to the fire, which burned slowly, hot coals glowing beneath the split oak logs Roger had placed on the fire. Violet sat in one of the chairs, with Roger on the floor beside her, his shoes off, long legs stretched out toward the warmth of the fire, an arm resting on her knees. Violet ran her hands caressingly through his short hair, and once she leaned forward and kissed the gray streaks showing vividly over his ears. For a long time, they were content to be together, touching; speech wasn't necessary. *Was this serenity and trust a preview of what their future might become?*

Eventually, Roger gently pulled Violet beside him on the braided rug, and they sat with their backs against the chair, his arm around her, and her head on his shoulder. Strange, how well her head fit into the curve of his neck! A light still burned in the kitchen, but where they sat, only the glowing coals provided any illumination.

"Yesterday," Roger said softly, "you told me something—I would like to hear it again."

"I love you, Roger."

"Yeah, I thought that's what you said." He turned toward her, putting both arms around her, nestling her close. It didn't seem at all strange for Violet to feel safe with him. She knew that no matter how much he desired her, Roger would never step across the line of moral decency—so when he kissed her she responded with an achingly sweet tenderness that matched his own.

"Obviously, we're in love," Roger said, and his voice trembled slightly, "so what are we going to do about it?"

"Yes, I love you," she said breathlessly. "I suppose I always have, and while this new emotion is the most exciting thing I've ever known, I'm still going to miss being friends.''

"My love will mean a lot more than mere friendship, but no man should marry a woman who isn't his friend. We'll always be friends—romantic love often wanes as couples grow older, friendship never does. And I guess I'm assuming that you will marry me.''

With a grin, Violet said, "I might, if I were asked.''

"I can't very well get down on my knees. I'm already sitting on the floor. But I do want to marry you, Violet. I've been thinking about it for a long time.''

"And I've only been thinking about it for a week, but it seems so right, Roger, that I don't really have to deliberate. I want to marry you, yet it isn't so simple. I'm alone, so that doesn't pose a problem.''

With a sigh, he said, "And I have two children to complicate our decision. How can I correlate my love and responsibility for them with my love for you? I've always thought that I wouldn't take a stepmother in while my children were still at home.''

"That might be a long time to wait.''

"I know, and I don't want to wait much longer. Jason is planning to backpack over Europe this summer, and when he returns, he will probably be going to the university. He won't be home much anymore, but Misty is only sixteen. She won't go to college for two years.''

"And while I don't feel any hesitancy about the difference in our ages…''

"Fourteen years,'' Roger groaned. "Don't think I haven't thought of it.''

"It does bother me,'' Violet continued, "that I'm not much older than your children.''

"The age difference bothers me, too, especially

when I think about having more children. You should have the privilege of having a child of your own, and I want to father your child, but I do have some reservations. At an age when I might become a grandfather, I'll be changing diapers again.''

"I've had good rapport with Jason and Misty in the classroom, but from teacher to stepmother is a vast step. I wonder what they will think about it?"

"There's only one way to know—ask them. With your permission, I intend to do that. If they aren't receptive to the idea, that doesn't mean I won't marry you, but it will complicate the situation. They're at home tonight—if you're willing, let's go and talk to them."

"So soon," Violet gasped. "I'll be nervous."

"Not as nervous as you'll be if you have several days to think about it."

Violet agreed hesitantly, and Roger said, "Now, what was that you told me earlier tonight? I may have forgotten."

She kissed her fingers and brushed them slowly across his lips. "I love you. How often do you have to hear it?"

"Oh, eventually, two or three times a day will suffice." He kissed her again, and she left his arms reluctantly. She wasn't looking forward to an interview with his children. It was much more pleasant to stay safely in his arms.

Chapter Six

Roger had built the ranch-style brick home soon after he had married. A two-car garage was attached to the house, and a row of evergreen hedges bordered the front of the building. Violet had never been to Roger's house, and her heart pounded unmercifully as they walked up the front steps; she was sustained only by Roger's strong grip on her hand. But she could sense his nervous tension as her side brushed against his— his body was as rigid as a stretched bow ready to release an arrow.

"Lord, help us," Roger prayed as he opened the door and led her into the hallway. They advanced a few feet into the living room where Jason and Misty were watching television. Jason was sprawled on the couch, Misty curled up in an upholstered chair. On the table between them was a big bowl of popcorn and a bottle of cola. The abrupt entrance of their father and Violet must have startled Misty and Jason for they looked inquiringly at the adults. When a few minutes passed and no one said anything, Jason muted the sound of the football game.

"Is something wrong?" Jason finally asked.

Roger cleared his throat, and struggling to speak, finally blurted out, "We want to get married."

Jason emitted a low, throaty laugh that sounded like his father's. "Well, get married. Who's to stop you? You're both old enough. Am I to understand you're asking our permission?"

Having gained some control, Roger tugged on Violet's hand and led her to another couch opposite the one where Jason lounged.

"We're not exactly asking your permission," Roger said slowly, "but we do think you deserve some consideration in the matter."

"You have my blessing," Jason said. "Misty?"

Misty sipped the cola she held. "I don't know," she said slowly. "I've always expected you to marry again, and I've worried a little about your being alone when Jason and I leave home. I suppose I just wasn't ready for it yet, but I'll get used to the idea—it's just a surprise."

"It came as a surprise to me, too," Violet said softly, speaking for the first time since their entrance.

With a slight grin, Misty said, "Oh, I'm not surprised that he asked *you*—I've known for a long time that you were the one he wanted."

"You have? Why am I the only one who didn't know it?"

"What's the matter with you, Dad?" Jason said as he sat upright on the couch. "I thought you could manage your romances better than that, or I would have advised you. 'Faint heart never won fair lady.'"

Roger's face flushed. "Cut it out, Jason. You're not making this easy for me."

"When are you expecting to get married?" Jason asked.

"In a year," Violet said, just as Roger said, "Six months."

Jason laughed uproariously. "I think you two had better get your act together and then come back and talk to us." He walked over to his father and placed a hand on his shoulder in a fatherly manner. "Decide what *you* want to do before you bring us into it. Rest assured that we'll give you all the advice you need."

Roger groaned and rolled his eyes upward. He stood and lifted Violet to a position beside him. To Misty, he said, "I take it, then, that you don't have any serious objections."

"No," she said slowly. "When Miss Conley is my teacher, I would feel funny about having her as a mother, but if you aren't married for six months *or* a year—" she smiled slightly "—I wouldn't be in her class then. You deserve to be happy, Dad. I know you've been lonely all these years that you've devoted your time to Jason and me. It's your turn for happiness now."

Roger leaned over and kissed Misty on the cheek. "I *have* been happy with just the three of us, but I love Violet, and I want her to become a part of our family."

Misty nodded, but she wouldn't look at him. Roger patted her bowed head. "I'll take Violet home and leave the two of you to your television."

The room was unusually quiet when they left, but Violet figured the two teenagers had plenty to say as soon as the door closed. When they entered the truck,

Violet leaned her head against the seat and exploded into laughter—uncontrollable laughter that erupted in waves of merriment.

"What's so amusing? I was scared to death."

"That was obvious, and we certainly presented an impressive spectacle to your children. I was shaking so much that I could hardly stand up, and you looked as if you were facing a firing squad."

"I would face death more calmly than I could confront those two kids. And, of course, Jason would choose to be facetious."

When Violet continued to laugh, he drew her toward him, "They're good kids, though," and Violet nodded her head against his shoulder. "That's the reason I don't want to do anything to hurt them."

He started the truck's engine and moved down the street. "It seems we have permission to set the date. Do you really want to wait a year?" Roger asked.

"I don't want to wait a week, but that's my heart talking. My common sense says we have to enter this slowly. A week ago I hadn't considered marrying you. We have to adjust to the idea slowly and give your children time to become reconciled to our marriage. For all their seeming acquiescence, it will initiate a big change in their lives. But, surely, six months would be long enough."

"Six months would be June 30. Would you like to be a June bride?"

"That sounds like a good idea. Schools will be closed for the summer, and Misty would no longer be my student. Let's plan on that date. The time will pass slowly, but there will be many decisions to make. For instance, will we keep my house and rent it, or sell it?"

"I realize that we do need to go slow, but the way I feel now, I want to take you over to Pastor Tom right away and have him perform an immediate ceremony to make us one."

Violet leaned over and kissed Roger's hand where it rested on the steering wheel.

"And speaking of Pastor Tom, I've decided to let him make an announcement about Mother's book. The popularity of that publication will go a long way toward erasing the stigma of her years in prison."

With the publication of the article, Violet felt a sense of closure over her mother's death, and she was optimistic about the future, even accepting the fact that she was going to be alone after Ruth's departure. She had never minded being by herself before, and one of the mixed blessings she looked forward to in marriage with Roger was that she would never be alone again. Already she could hardly bear to be separated from him, so that didn't trouble her much, but she did wonder how she would deal with having two children in the house. On the plus side, she remembered how she had longed for a big family during her childhood, and she realized that she would be obtaining not only a husband, but an instant family, when she and Roger married.

After the article had been published, she sensed a difference in the attitude of her acquaintances. One day she saw Mrs. Holland riding along in her chauffeured limousine, and she had graciously lifted her hand. Even Larry was making overtures to her again, and though she treated him civilly, she wondered if he thought she would fall into his arms after his desertion during her time of greatest need. Apparently no one was aware that she intended to marry Roger, for they hadn't made public announcement of their engagement, and Misty and Jason must not have mentioned it, either. She couldn't imagine that any of her acquaintances could be unaware of the time she and Roger spent together, but no comments were made.

When the new semester started, Janie Skeen enrolled in two art classes, and the instructor reported to Violet that the girl had a natural aptitude for sketching. Janie had started attending the youth group at First Community Church, and she had made new friends there—friendships that carried over to Maitland High, where she was more accepted socially. Violet wondered frequently if Janie's father had discovered where his daughter lived.

Most of the worries that had been plaguing Violet for the past few months were dissipating and she anticipated her future with gladness. But the day before Ruth left, Violet received a disturbing letter. She had been lulled into a sense of complacency, thinking that the future held no surprises, although she should have known better. God had helped her through the trying days of her mother's illness and death, and she was looking forward to the future with much anticipation, knowing that nothing could happen now that she couldn't handle with God's help. Even after she read the letter, she wasn't as disconsolate as she had been when she had received the message about her mother's prison release, a sign of spiritual maturation on her part.

Violet found it difficult to comprehend the content of the terse message, and she handed it to Ruth who read it aloud.

"I have learned that my grandson, Mike Conley,

encountered you recently. I have made enough
investigation to know that you are my granddaughter, born to my son, Ryan Conley. Please
call upon me as soon as possible. Telephone my
secretary at the number below when you expect
to arrive.

Josiah B. Conley,
Kansas City, Kansas''

"There's no doubt the letter is from your grandfather," Ruth said with a grimace. "Always the exalted
potentate giving orders to his subjects." She tapped
the message significantly. "That paints a picture of
what he's like, and how he was able to railroad your
mother into prison. Are you going to obey the sum-
mons?"

"Of course not," Violet said. "Do you think I
should?"

"No, although I am curious about what he wants.
No doubt, he's heard of Linda's death."

"Something just occurred to me. Why didn't the
Conleys take me when my mother was sent to
prison?"

"That's some of the information you can learn from
William O'Brien, but with all of the trouble Linda had
with the Conleys, she wouldn't have wanted you to
live with them."

When Roger came that evening to bid Ruth goodbye, Violet showed him the letter.

"He doesn't sound like a doting grandfather,"
Roger said with a laugh.

"My husband and I were in Mexico during the
years that Linda and Ryan were married," Ruth said,
"so I haven't met any of the Conleys. My husband

was an archeologist, and we were isolated on a dig during the time of the trial. Violet lived with Linda's attorney and his wife for a few months until we returned, and I took her into our home. Even in her letters, Linda didn't have much to say about her in-laws, but enough to indicate that Josiah Conley dominated the lives of his two sons.''

"Are you going?'' Roger asked as he handed the letter back to Violet.

"I have a strange feeling about this, as if I don't have any business mixing with the Conleys. They evidently brought about my mother's downfall. I'm better off ignoring them.''

But in the end, she answered the letter, addressing it to "Mr. Conley,'' for she wouldn't recognize him as her grandfather. She wrote, "If you had me investigated, then you will know that I'm employed as a public schoolteacher, and I have a busy schedule. I will have some vacation during the Easter Holidays, and if I should have occasion to be in Kansas City during that time, I will contact you.''

It was still six weeks before Easter, and Violet thought she would not have to worry about seeing her grandfather until then, and she could devote more thought to her marriage and the decisions she and Roger must make. Her ship of life was sailing smoothly again, and she didn't want the Conleys to disrupt that. Then a second jolt penetrated her horizon.

Violet was unaware that the Associated Press had picked up the article about her mother's book and subsequent death until she received a visitor late one afternoon. Ever afterward, she believed God had placed Roger in her home that day, for she needed him beside her when she first met Peter Pierce. Roger had arrived soon after she came from school, for they wanted to assess the value of her house, and decide if any repairs should be made before they reached a decision about putting the house on the market for sale or rent. A cold March wind offset the sun's warmth as they walked around in the backyard, and Roger looked over the exterior siding. He had just descended the ladder, after checking out the roof and the guttering, when they heard a car stop in the driveway.

Violet walked around the house to check on her visitor. A black van with a New York license was parked behind her car, and a man, who looked somewhat familiar, was exiting the vehicle, a briefcase in his hand. He saw her, and with a broad smile, walked in her direction.

"Miss Conley," he said. "Miss Violet Conley?"

Roger had joined her by that time. "Yes," she answered.

"I'm Peter Pierce," the stranger said, "Perhaps you've heard of me."

No wonder he seemed familiar—her visitor was the emcee of the hit program, "Travesty of Justice," that aired on a major network every Saturday night. Violet hadn't watched his show often, but she did remember one program that had cleared the name of a convict executed in the electric chair—a few years too late someone else had confessed to the crime.

"Yes, I've heard of you."

He presented a card for identification, but none was really needed, for his face was well-known to television viewers. Pierce looked questioningly at Roger, and Violet said, "This is my fiancé, Roger Gibson."

Pierce shook hands with Roger. "I'd like to talk

with you, Miss Conley, if you can spare a half hour of your time.''

''I suppose so.'' Violet glanced at Roger.

''I suppose we can speak with him Violet,'' Roger said.

She opened the door and the two men followed her into the kitchen. ''May I offer you a soft drink, Mr. Pierce?''

''That would be fine.''

''Let's sit here at the dining table, then. The bright sun is making this alcove a pleasant spot right now.''

Roger took three glasses from the cabinet, Violet filled them with a lemon-lime drink, and the three of them sat at the table.

''I will come to the reason for my visit right away.'' He opened his briefcase and took out a folder, from which he extracted a newspaper clipping. When he handed it to her, Violet saw that it was the article about her mother that had appeared in the *Maitland News*.

''If you've watched our telecast, you know that we are dedicated to righting the wrongs of juries, who in ignorance or by design, have brought judgments against innocent people. This article was forwarded to us by a reader, who had read your mother's book, suggesting that Linda Conley's conviction would be a good subject for one of our investigations. After I read the article, I was inclined to agree that the story would make a good feature for our program, and I've spent the past few days in Kansas City, delving into the records of your mother's trial and conviction. I don't believe the full story was ever told, but I received no cooperation from your mother's attorney, William

O'Brien. He said he wouldn't even talk to us about the trial without your permission."

"Since I've been hesitant to learn the truth for myself, I'm not inclined to allow her story to be aired nationwide. My mother told me nothing about the incident—she obviously didn't want any publicity about it, so I doubt that I would ever agree to any broadcast."

"I'm authorized to offer you $500,000 for first rights on this story," he said, his confident tone indicating that the high figure would sway Violet's opinion.

"Money will have nothing to do with my decision."

"Then you will consider it?"

Violet looked at Roger. "What do you think?"

He smiled and took her hand. "The same as I've told you before on other matters. Don't make a hasty decision. Mr. Pierce is eager to get your name on the dotted line before someone else approaches you, but you don't have to give him your answer today."

"We'll top any offer you receive," Pierce said. "The story intrigues me."

"You think I'll be approached by others?" Violet said in amazement.

Pierce nodded his head emphatically. "Undoubtedly. Someone is going to publish this story, with or without your approval, and you will benefit from having it done by a reputable producer like ours, rather than to have Linda Conley's experience aired with half truths, innuendoes, and downright lies."

Roger nodded in agreement.

"Under no circumstances will I agree to the broadcast until I know the truth. I may go to Kansas City during the Easter Holidays, and if so, I will contact Mr. O'Brien. When I learn the story, I'll consider your offer."

"Will you promise me that you won't negotiate with anyone else before then—that you will give me first refusal?"

Violet looked at Roger, and he shook his head. "I wouldn't tie myself to any commitment." His eyes sparkled. "At least, not anything of this nature."

She knew he was thinking of her commitment to marry him, and his bit of humor helped when she said, "I'll agree to contact you with my decision between Easter and the first of May—I can't promise you more than that."

"Of course, there's a possibility that we might want to withdraw the offer before then."

"That's all right," Violet said. "Such an action would simply indicate that God didn't want me to grant permission. In the meantime, I'll be praying for guidance on whether I should deal with you at all."

Graciously, but with a hint of frustration, Peter Pierce left.

"I'm glad you were here, Roger," Violet said. "Since I believe God is guiding my decisions as always, it seems that I'm getting more and more reasons to go to Kansas City."

Roger stood to leave, for his hour was almost over. "It does seem that way." He pulled her into his arms, where she snuggled contentedly. "Do you want me to go with you?"

"Yes, of course, but I won't let you. I'll probably be gone most of the week, and you should be with Misty when she has her vacation week."

He sighed. "I know—now my first responsibility is

to Misty and Jason, but before too long, I'll have the right to make you my major priority.'' He bent to kiss her and Violet's hands clasped around his neck. With a sigh he gently broke the embrace and went out to his truck.

Wondering if William O'Brien would still be in his office, Violet found his telephone number in the estate correspondence and dialed. A secretary answered, Violet gave her name, and she was soon talking to O'Brien. She explained about her visit from Peter Pierce.

''I was sure he would come to see you, and perhaps I should have warned you. What have you decided?''

''That I want to find out the truth before I agree to the documentary.''

''That is a wise move.''

''I may be in Kansas City the week after Easter, and if so, would you have time to talk with me? Mother left it to my discretion to learn about her conviction—she said you would tell me.''

''I will be pleased to serve you as I tried to serve your mother.''

''You might be interested in the other reason I have for coming to Kansas City. My grandfather contacted me by letter, practically demanding that I come to see him.''

''You mean old Josiah Conley wants to see you?''

''That's what his letter indicated.''

''I can't imagine what that old varmint wants. If I were you, I wouldn't go near him. I don't know what he wants, but I can assure you that it isn't anything for your benefit. But if you do come to Kansas City, let me know what days you will want to see me, for it may take more than a day if you delve very deeply into your mother's past.''

A light mist was falling the day after Easter when Violet set out for Kansas City, but the heavy clouds soon turned into feathery wisps, and the sun broke through. She tried to enjoy the scenery, but her mind was too befuddled with what was facing her in the coming week.

Violet had written to Josiah B. Conley that she would be in Kansas City on Tuesday, and that she could call upon him if he so desired. His secretary telephoned that Mr. Conley would see her at ten o'clock, Tuesday, at his residence, and she gave the address. On Wednesday, she would see William O'Brien at his office. The rest of the week was unplanned.

It was late afternoon when she reached the hotel where she had reserved a room. She waited until after dinner before she telephoned Roger, as he had asked her to do. In answer to his question, she said, ''The drive was uneventful, but I'm feeling lonely tonight. Kansas City is a big place, and I don't know anyone here.''

''I'm lonely, too. Knowing that you aren't in Maitland makes it an empty town.''

''Before too long, we can be together all the time. Does that prospect appeal to you?''

''Seventy-five more days!'' Roger said with his slow laugh. ''I'm checking them off on the calendar.''

If she hadn't been so apprehensive about what the next few days held, Violet could have gone to sleep content in the confidence of Roger's love and their future together. As it was, she felt alone, isolated from everyone she knew, although she knew that Roger and Aunt Ruth were as close as the phone. But as she lay in bed wooing sleep, she was comforted by the knowledge that she was never separated from God, that He was present with her at all times, and it didn't even require a phone call to contact Him. Her loneliness was eased by the realization that when the Spirit of God lived within her, she need never feel lonely.

Violet tried to remember a Scripture passage that Pastor Tom had quoted in his sermon yesterday, but when she could not, she switched on the light and reached into the nightstand drawer for a New Testament. The Good News interpretation from the fourteenth chapter of John was particularly meaningful in her situation: "I will ask the Father, and he will give you another Helper, the Spirit of truth, to stay with you for ever.... You know him, for he remains with you and lives in you. I will not leave you alone."

In the sermon, Pastor Tom had stressed the loneliness that came upon Jesus's followers after He was crucified, but following His resurrection, they remembered the many times Jesus had assured them that He would never leave them. The disciples had endured persecution and imprisonment, and they probably felt forsaken in their prison cells, but as they stood before their accusers, those words of Jesus, that they might not have understood at the time, would have brought joy to their hearts and courage to their wills: *I will not leave you alone.*

"Thank you, God, for giving me the assurance through Your son, Jesus, and the Spirit dwelling within, that whatever I face this week, Your Spirit will be with me."

Chapter Seven

Knowing nothing about Kansas City, Violet took a taxi to the Conleys. After a short drive from her hotel, the taxi passed through the gateway of a white iron fence that surrounded a huge house, and drove slowly along the circular driveway to stop in front of curved steps leading to a portico that sheltered double doors.

The graceful pink Georgian mansion had stood there for several years, for Kansas City had grown up around the property, which must have been at least three acres. The central part of the house encompassed three floors, with two one-story wings flanking the larger portion. The elegance of the house was emphasized by graceful, symmetrical lines. Violet was stunned at the magnificence of the place.

She paid the taxi driver and could hardly stand erect when she stepped out of the taxi. Concluding that she might be under observation by the house's occupants, she straightened her back and walked as briskly as possible up the three curved steps and stopped under the portico. Violet rang the doorbell and waited nervously until the door was opened by a black-eyed young woman in a dark dress.

"Miss Conley?" she said.

"I'm Violet Conley."

With a smile the young woman indicated that Violet should enter. Stepping into the house, Violet entered a new world. A grand staircase dominated the entrance hall, and on one side of the spacious hall, Violet saw a large dining room, with a crystal chandelier hanging over a shining mahogany table. A formal living area was on the opposite side of the hall.

"The living quarters are on the second floor. Please follow me," the maid said, and she walked smartly up a stairway lined with portraits, and stopped on the balcony affording a view of the lower hall.

"Please be seated in the library, and I'll tell Mr. Conley that you've arrived." She ushered Violet into a room finished in cherry paneling, where two sides were lined with bookshelves, and another wall dominated by a marble fireplace. It was inconceivable that Violet Conley's father had lived in such opulence.

Violet wouldn't have been surprised if she had been left waiting a long time, because she was a few minutes early, but the maid returned quickly and motioned Violet to follow her down the hallway. She opened the door into a combination office and sitting room that overlooked a broad lawn, and Violet had the first glimpse of her grandfather sitting behind a walnut desk that seemed too big for him. *This is the man who sent my mother to prison.*

Josiah Conley was not a tall man, and his flesh hung loosely on his sparse frame. He was seated when she entered, but he stared at her with incredulous eyes, and stood as though he were in a trance. The words he uttered were the last ones she would have expected from this man who had caused her disastrous childhood.

His voice was warm and friendly, as he tenderly whispered, "Oh, my dear, I had no idea... You are the image of your grandmother—my wife, Rachel—when she was your age."

He motioned toward a large portrait over the fireplace, and Violet saw her own face staring down at her. Without an invitation, she sank weakly into the nearest chair.

Josiah Conley seemed even smaller when he stood, but with brown eyes gleaming below a thatch of snow-white hair, he came to Violet and took her hand. "There's no doubt that you are the offspring of my son, Ryan. I was fearful to contact you even when my investigators proved who you were, but you walk in, and it's almost like having my Rachel back with me. I've been worrying about the future of this family, and here you are."

Violet looked at him in surprise and dismay. She had never met anyone who displayed such a dominant personality, or one who exuded absolute control. Josiah Conley went to his desk and spoke into the intercom. An adjoining door opened, and a middle-aged woman entered to stand beside the desk.

"Miss Whitaker, this is my granddaughter, Violet. Please arrange for her to eat lunch and spend the rest of the day with us. Order a room readied for her. We can have her luggage brought from the hotel later on, but she will need a place to change before the reception tonight."

"Now just a minute," Violet said. "I have other

plans for my week. Don't make any arrangements for me. I'm perfectly happy at the hotel.''

Josiah didn't heed her words. ''And, Miss Whitaker, please go out and buy a suitable garment for her to wear to the reception this evening. She and I have business to discuss this afternoon, and she won't have time for shopping. Also, stop at the bank and bring my wife's jewelry from the vault.''

Miss Whitaker turned her attention to Violet. ''And what size garment do you wear, Miss Conley?''

''I don't want you to buy any clothing for me!''

''I can judge her size well enough,'' Miss Whitaker said to Josiah, as her eaglelike eyes scanned every part of Violet's person while she made notations on the pad she carried. ''Those shoes won't do for a formal evening. What is your shoe size?''

Violet's face flushed. ''Size seven, narrow,'' she said grudgingly.

After Miss Whitaker left the room, Violet said, ''What reception? Even if I do attend, I can afford to buy my own clothing.''

Josiah ignored her last comment. ''You came on a very important day. This evening, I'm hosting a reception for the man who may very well be the next president of the United States. He's been my business associate for several years, and he's making his candidacy announcement tonight. I've been without a hostess since my Rachel died, and I want you to stand with me in the receiving line tonight. There will be nearly one hundred people here.''

''None of whom I will know,'' she said. Josiah waved away her objection, and although she didn't like to be manipulated, she had nothing else to do until she went to see O'Brien tomorrow. It might be enlightening to meet the next president. "If I can be of any help to you, I will stay until after the reception, but I have plans for the rest of the week."

"Wait until you hear my proposition, and you may be willing to forgo any plans you have and turn your future over to me." He returned to his desk and motioned her to a chair nearby. "Come, let me be frank with you."

Violet perched on the chair he indicated, wanting nothing more than to bolt out of the room and rush back to Roger in Maitland. Josiah kept looking at her and then glancing at the portrait of his wife, and his smile broadened with each glance, making Violet extremely uncomfortable. She looked at the portrait once again and was alarmed by the many personal resemblances she recognized. If the artist's conception of Mrs. Conley was true, she had inherited her grandmother's facial expressions, coloring and hair color. It was heartening to note that Rachel did not have violet eyes. At least that was one facial characteristic she could call her own. Dressed in garments of a few decades before, her grandmother looked down on Violet with mysterious blue eyes, as if she had secrets that not even the artist could discern.

She turned her back on the portrait, but it was uncanny to feel that every move she made was observed by those inscrutable eyes. She shouldn't have come here—she felt like a cornered animal, waiting for the predator to attack. *I will not leave you alone.*

"Violet, as you may know, I am a very wealthy man, but riches aren't everything. My beloved wife and my two sons are dead—their only issue one grandson and a granddaughter. You met my grandson, Mike, a few months ago. In spite of my urging, he has lived a profligate life and has refused to marry. Now, he's dying, and I thought my hopes of establishing a Conley empire were dying with him, until he told me about you. I had no idea what had happened to you.''

''As I understand, the Conleys weren't interested in me or my mother, and she didn't want you to know where I was. That's the reason my aunt took me to another state to live.''

''Your mother was a vindictive person.''

''Not when I knew her—and that has been the past few months when she was dying.''

Josiah didn't pay any attention to her remark. ''I was delighted to know that you had turned out well and lived a respectable life, and now knowing that you resemble Rachel, my plans are bound to succeed. A more wonderful woman never lived than my wife.''

The telephone jangled softly, Josiah peered at the caller ID machine and severed the connection without answering. Looking at the clock, he said, ''It's time for lunch now. We'll continue this discussion after we've eaten.''

They ate in a small dining room in one of the wings, and even that table was large enough to accommodate ten or twelve people. With Violet sitting at one end of the long table, and Josiah at the other, their conversation was limited during the serving of a salad course, hot mushroom soup and poached salmon with dill sauce. Toasted bread accompanied the soup. A lemon sorbet was served for dessert.

In the background, Violet heard the hum of activity as caterers and florists prepared the mansion for the coming reception. After they had eaten, Josiah called the maid who had admitted her to the house earlier.

''Will you show Violet to the room you've prepared

for her, and in a half hour bring her down to my office? You will help her dress and provide what she needs before the reception this evening.''

She followed the maid up the central stairway and turned toward one of the wings, where the maid opened a door and bowed for Violet to enter. Violet perceived at once that she was in Rachel Conley's bedroom, and she inquired of the maid.

''It is her bedroom. I have been here only two years, so I do not remember Mrs. Conley, but I understand that the room is kept exactly as it was the day she died. Nothing has been removed from the room. You are to rest—I will return in a half hour.''

Violet wondered if Josiah decreed when one could, or could not, rest in his house. The maid went out and softly closed the door, and feeling like a trapped animal, Violet stood with her back against the wall and looked at the room's furnishings. Carpet, draperies, and bedspread were fashioned in soft pink fabrics. The bed, chest and dresser were painted in ivory. A chaise lounge stood near the double windows, and a pair of house slippers were beside it.

On the dresser were brushes, mirrors and a cosmetic case. Family pictures covered the top of the chest of drawers—most were of Josiah, Rachel and their two sons when they were boys. There were some individual pictures of the sons grown to manhood, and Violet walked over and picked up one which must be her father because he looked like Rachel's portrait. The other son had the features of Josiah. There was only one wedding portrait—that of Josiah and Rachel. It was understandable that Rachel would not want a wedding photo of Violet's parents, but one would have thought there would be a picture of Mike's mother. A few baby pictures must have been of Mike, but she found none of herself.

Violet opened the closet to find it full of clothing. Josiah had made this room into a shrine, and Violet had an eerie feeling about it all. She opened the double windows and walked out on the small balcony, to observe the rear lawn that was spacious and landscaped with variously shaped flower beds that must have the flowers changed according to the season. Right now, daffodils, hyacinths and tulips bloomed in profusion. Small tables were being set up around the lawn in preparation for the evening.

Violet hadn't rested at all when the maid came to conduct her back to Josiah's office. Violet monitored her surroundings as she strolled along. The house was so large she could easily lose her way, and if she wanted to leave in a hurry, she wanted to know how to exit the place.

Josiah received her with a smile, seated her in a plush chair, and came quickly to his reason for summoning her to Kansas City. "I will have one of my lawyers present before we make final arrangements, but this is just a preliminary discussion. As I told you, I've acquired a vast fortune, and I have no desire for strangers to reap the benefits of my labor. I rebel at giving my fortune to charity. I want you to come here to live, marry and have children who will someday inherit my vast holdings. I will also make generous bequests to you personally."

Her hand pulled at the collar of her blouse as she stared at him, and he dropped his eyelids under her intense violet gaze.

"I can easily arrange a suitable marriage for you, or do you have someone in mind?"

"I'm engaged—we plan to marry June 30."

"He will probably do just as well as anyone to father your children. What's his name?"

"Roger Gibson," she said shortly. "He lives in Maitland—he's an Illinois state policeman."

Josiah scribbled Roger's name on a pad at his side. "I'll check on him. If he has any administrative ability, we can fit him easily into Midwest Enterprises. Of course, I would want him to take the Conley name, but if he still wants to retain his name, you could become Conley-Gibson." He tried the name on his tongue again. "Conley-Gibson. That has a nice sound."

He paused, and Violet said hurriedly, "Has it occurred to you that I might not be interested in coming to Kansas City? I have a good job, and when Roger and I marry, we intend to settle down in Maitland. I'm sure Roger would not do what you want. Your generosity is appreciated, but you must look someplace else for an heir."

"If this Roger of yours is smart enough to warrant being your husband, I'm sure he will advise you to accept my offer. Not many men would be so foolish as to turn down a fortune and security for their own children."

Violet couldn't believe that Roger was interested in wealth, but he might be willing to listen to Josiah's proposition. She knew he was concerned about providing for a new family when he had Misty and Jason to educate. The thought of living in this household made her feel creepy, but should Roger have the opportunity to speak for himself? With Roger beside her, Josiah Conley might seem less formidable.

But Violet wouldn't concede anything to this man

before her. "We are both actively involved in our church work in Maitland, and we wouldn't want to leave our spiritual family."

Josiah waved a hand, negligibly disregarding her concern. "I've never had time for church myself, though Rachel used to go, but there's a church on every corner in Kansas City. Choose any one you want, and I'll endow it. That way, you and your husband can be elected to important offices. We'll choose a church with many influential members."

His audacity angered Violet, but she also felt like laughing aloud. His suggestions for choosing a church were ludicrous, and she wondered how to deal with him. Before the afternoon passed, Violet was aware that one could neither argue nor reason with her grandfather. In a grudging way, she liked the man, but she was afraid of him. After being in his overwhelming presence for a few hours, her willpower was gone, and by evening, she had lost the mental strength to contend with him.

When she returned to her room, a black, floor-length silk dress overlaid with lace was spread out on the bed. Sweat popped out on Violet's body when she read the name of a famous French designer on the label—the cost of this one garment would provide her normal clothing budget for several years. It was no wonder that Josiah had disregarded her remark that she could buy her own clothing!

Violet submitted to the ministrations of the French maid as she arranged her hair, applied makeup, and dropped the shimmering black dress over her head. A dainty train flowed behind her as she walked around the room to test the length of the garment. The dress was sleeveless and the neckline much too low for Violet's comfort, but the maid produced a set of finger-less black lace gloves that came to the elbow. Violet sat on the lounge and stretched out her feet for the maid to put on the decorative slingback shoes covered with tiny cube-shaped rhinestones.

A knock sounded at the door, and Miss Whitaker entered carrying a large chest. She opened the chest to display five drawers of jewels. Violet could only stare at the ostentatious jewelry that reminded her of the Crown jewels.

"Your grandfather wants you to choose something from his wife's jewelry to wear to the reception to-night."

Finding her voice, Violet said, "I don't want to wear this jewelry—what if I should lose it?"

Miss Whitaker's straight lips wrinkled into a half smile. "Hardly any danger of losing anything in this house tonight. There will be numerous security agents circulating."

Desperately, Violet protested, "I still don't want to wear them. In fact, I don't even want to go to the reception."

In her way, Miss Whitaker was as domineering as Josiah Conley, Violet decided, for she ignored Violet's comments and turned her so that she faced the mirror. The secretary lifted a gold necklace set with rubies and diamonds and placed it around Violet's neck.

"This is probably a good choice," she said. "It's certainly not the most expensive necklace Mrs. Conley owned, but it does look stunning with that dress." She clasped the necklace around Violet's neck, removed the simple gold earrings from Violet's ears and in-serted the long pendants that matched the necklace. She unwrapped a matching bracelet and gave it to Violet to put over her wrist, while she rummaged carefully in the lower drawer containing a dozen or so rings. Violet's hands were ringless, so Miss Whitaker placed a large diamond solitaire on her left hand, and a diamond encrusted circlet on the third finger of her right hand. Chills coursed through Violet's body when she realized that the rings fit perfectly.

Miss Whitaker took a box from one drawer of the chest. "This was your grandmother's favorite necklace, which she inherited from her forebears. Note especially the golden loop-in-loop chain work."

The necklace was hung with rose-shaped pendants, highlighted by gold-and-silver enamel, and it was beautiful. The secretary replaced the necklace in the box and locked the chest.

"Come along now," Miss Whitaker said. "Let's see if Mr. Conley approves your appearance, and I must lock this jewelry in the safe."

As they hustled down the hall, Violet observed her appearance in a floor-length mirror. Only her hair looked normal, and because it was so short, the maid couldn't change it much. That fact gave Violet some comfort—how could a designer dress and expensive jewelry do so much to alter one's appearance? She would have to be on guard, or it would change her personality as well.

When Miss Whitaker opened the door and ushered Violet into Josiah's office, he stood to his feet, his expression awestruck.

"Magnificent!" he said. "I have my Rachel back again." He favored her with such a possessive look that Violet's blood chilled. Would he try to force her to remain in this house?

"Then you approve?" Miss Whitaker said.

"Very much. You have done well." To Violet, he said, "We will dine in a half hour."

"Then may I suggest," Miss Whitaker said, "that you hurry to change your own garments."

"Point well taken," Josiah said. He patted Violet on her shoulder, and she was repulsed by the gesture.

Back in her room, Violet was left alone for a few minutes, and ignoring her finery, she knelt by the chaise lounge. "God," she prayed, "I'm in a situation that I can't control, and one that terrifies me. What am I going to do?" While she knelt with her head on the lounge, she thought of Rachel Conley, whose presence seemed to fill the room. "Grandmother," Violet said, not believing that Rachel could hear her, but she did feel an affinity to that grandmother she couldn't remember, "if I'm like you as I've been led to believe, there must have been times when you were frightened and uneasy in this house. I hope I can be as composed as you must have been."

As she remained on her knees waiting for God's answer, He answered her as she recalled some words from *What's Your Prison?* Linda had written, "There is no dungeon so deep, no prison wall so secure to prevent God from reaching out to His children. Paul and Silas prayed in the Philippian jail and were heard; Jonah prayed from the belly of the big fish and God answered; though Joseph had reached the depths of Potiphar's dungeon, he was delivered; and even when Jeremiah was in the dungeon, God protected and strengthened the prophet to continue his God-given work. Be encouraged—if you belong to God, you will never be in any situation from which He can't deliver you. It may be that He will send angels to guard you,

or perhaps deliverance will come by your own ingenuity, but be assured, wherever you are, God is there.''

Such peace flowed into Violet's soul that she
praised God for delivering her from the dread of this
evening. And how wonderful that her comfort had
come through her mother's words. Linda, of all people, would understand how Violet felt tonight. She had
been intimidated by Josiah long before Violet was
born.

Violet was still on her knees, resting her head on
the lounge, when the door opened, and the maid
screeched, *"Mademoiselle!"* The woman rushed to
Violet and lifted her up to her feet.

"What is the matter? You have wrinkled your
dress.''

"Nothing is the matter...now. And there isn't anything wrong with my dress," Violet added, as the maid
tugged at the garment and brushed away a few specks
of lint she had picked up from the pink carpet.

During the dinner, which was served to a group of
about thirty guests, Violet kept encountering the sar-
donic glances of a man who sat about halfway down
the table on her left. He seemed familiar to her. At
last, she placed him—Mike Conley, Josiah's grandson,
whom she had met at the Social Studies competition
in Springfield. She wondered how she felt about her
elevation to such an exalted position. She remembered
Josiah's comment that his grandson was terminally ill.
Violet had thought Mike Conley looked pale and hag-
gard at the first meeting and now he looked even more
sickly. Clearly, his health was rapidly deteriorating.

There was a half-hour break between dinner and the
beginning of the reception, and Violet left the dining

room, hoping she could find her way back to Rachel's bedroom. Mike Conley blocked her way when she entered the hallway.

"So we meet again," he said. "And you've been ignoring me when I thought you would be grateful—without my intervention, you wouldn't have been invited into these exclusive halls."

"I didn't recognize you at first, but believe me, I'm not grateful that you told your grandfather of my existence. He practically ordered me to come to see him, and when I came, he wouldn't let me leave. I feel like a prisoner."

"Which you really are. Josiah has always imprisoned members of his family."

"But if you think I'm happy in such a gathering as this, you're mistaken. Nothing personal, but I'm sorry that you and I encountered each other."

"I know it wasn't a kind thing for me to do, but dare I admit, that I told him about you to get him off my back for a while. He didn't seem to understand that I wasn't the one to carry on his kingdom. I'd just about run out of the strength to oppose him when you appeared on the horizon."

"I'm surprised that you would want to take a chance on him leaving some of his possessions to me."

"I inherited my father's share of Midwest Enterprises—I have more money than I can ever spend in the short time I have left."

"I'm not sure I'm interested in carrying on his legacy, either."

He looked at her keenly. "You mean that, don't you?" He indicated the spacious house with a sweep of his hand. "This hasn't impressed you at all."

"Until a few weeks ago, all I ever knew about the Conleys was that they had railroaded my mother into prison and left me without any parental guidance. My mother wouldn't see me, and my Aunt Ruth answered few questions, but enough for me to realize that I was better off not knowing anything about my father's people."

"Josiah won't give up without a fight," Mike warned her.

"I need to get away from him so I can think. He acts as if the decision is already made, but I don't think my fiancé will be interested in his proposition."

"Are you engaged to the man who was with you in Springfield?"

"Yes, we plan to be married in June, and I doubt he will be interested in my grandfather's offer, but I do think he should be considered in my decision."

"He appeared to be a good man."

"He is," Violet said, and her face wreathed into a smile; even the thought of Roger brought her pleasure.

"Then you should forget Midwest Enterprises and stay with him."

"My opinion exactly. That's why I intend to leave as soon as the reception is over."

Mike shook his head. "Maybe not. I've already had my orders to drive you back to your hotel tonight and bring you and your luggage back here to stay."

"No! No!" Violet grabbed his arm. "You're the one who got me into this, so please help me. Take me away now."

Mike rubbed his forehead, as if thinking was too painful for him. "It isn't that easy to evade Josiah's clutches, but let me think upon it, and I'll do something for you."

Miss Whitaker appeared behind them and Violet wondered what she had heard.

"Your grandfather is expecting the two of you to join him in the front hallway in five minutes."

"Then we will have to hurry, Violet. We mustn't keep grandfather waiting."

He gave her a significant nod and wandered away. Lifting the front hem of her dress and letting the train flow behind her, Violet rushed up the back stairs to Rachel's bedroom. She had to have a few moments to herself before she faced all of those strangers.

The massive looped earrings pulled on Violet's earlobes, and the necklace felt cold and heavy on her neck. Again Violet got a glimpse of herself in the floor-length mirror as she hurried along the carpeted hall. Outwardly, she appeared more beautiful than she had ever looked before, but she didn't look like herself, and with the addition of all the finery, her personality had disappeared. She couldn't even remember the values and goals of the Violet Conley she had once been. If one day in her grandfather's presence could do that, how would a daily diet of his dominance affect her? It was unthinkable.

She endured the rest of the evening, standing at his side as he proudly introduced her to his acquaintances. When all the guests had assembled, and Josiah was busy with the presidential contender, standing beside him as he made his bid for the country's highest office, Mike appeared at her side.

"Go upstairs and gather your things. In five minutes I'll knock on the door and guide you to the servants' exit, where a taxi is supposed to be waiting for you. You would never be able to escape being seen if you go out any of the other doors."

She searched his eyes for a few moments. Could she trust him? Somehow she thought that she could, and she knew that she had to leave this place before she lost her small amount of remaining mental ingenuity. In the bedroom she changed out of the expensive dress into the slacks outfit she had worn to the house, removed the jewelry and laid it on top of the dress, hoping nothing would happen to it before Miss Whitaker could return it in the safe.

Violet was ready when she heard a discreet knock on the door, and without a word, she followed Mike down a small set of stairs. He opened the outside door and looked around before he motioned her to exit. A taxi stood beside the steps.

"Thank you, Mike. I hope you won't get in trouble because of this."

"Don't worry about me—I can't sink any lower in my grandfather's estimation." He took her hand. "I think I would have enjoyed knowing you as a cousin. I had a lonely childhood with no other children around."

"So did I. I guess that tragedy with my parents ruined both of our lives."

"The tragedy was that both of us were born Conleys." He opened the taxi door for her and squeezed her hand. "Watch out for yourself. Good luck."

When the taxi pulled up before her hotel, Violet asked the driver to wait. She went inside, checked out of her room, and directed the taxi driver to take her to another hotel. Knowing her grandfather's investigative powers, she registered as Ruth Reed, and by paying for the room in advance with cash, she didn't have to present any identification cards. She checked into her room, and only then did she rid herself of the feeling that Josiah would snatch her back into his fold.

Right now, she needed Roger, and she dialed his number, thankful that she found him at home and not out on special duty. After they chatted about inconsequentials, she said, "Would you like to become an instant millionaire?"

"What's the catch?" Roger asked in a teasing tone.

"I went to see my grandfather today, and he wants to make me his heir. His only other direct descendant is that grandson I told you about. Sadly, the poor man is dying."

"That's unfortunate," Roger replied. "So you would be the only heir." Roger's voice was wary. "You sound excited."

She wanted to tell him of how Josiah had dominated her, but no need to worry him when he was too far away to do anything.

"I've had quite a day, and certainly his offer is generous, but you're included, too. He wants me to marry and have children to eventually carry on his business of Midwest Enterprises. When I told him I was engaged, he said he would welcome you and give you a job in the corporation. There's one catch, though."

"There usually is," he said with a light laugh.

"We would have to move to Kansas City, live in the family home, and change your name to Conley, or at least I would need to retain my family name in our marriage. How does Roger Conley-Gibson sound to you?"

"Sounds as if you're making up the whole thing to tease me."

"No, I'm serious. I've spent the afternoon out there listening to him."

"That's a situation you will have to ponder carefully," Roger said slowly. *Was his voice strained, or did she imagine it?*

"But you would be involved, too."

"Oh, I don't think so."

"I can't make any decision without considering you, Roger."

He ignored her comment, saying only, "What you decide could change your whole life, so think on it carefully."

"Will you pray for me, Roger? It seems all I've done in the past few months is to make decisions."

After she told him she had shifted hotels, without giving him a reason, she added, "I love you," and said goodbye. She had never wanted his presence with her so much as she did when she finally got into bed, even then dreading a call from her grandfather. Again lonely, and somewhat fearful without Roger, she relied on the promise, *I will not leave you alone.*

Chapter Eight

William O'Brien's office was in a long ell attached to his two-story redbrick house, that looked as if had been built several years ago because the shrubbery and trees on the small lot were well established. Although she hadn't seen O'Brien, her telephone conversations with him had proven that he was not only a capable man, but one who seemingly had compassion for his clients.

Violet had taken a taxi to his office, and when she entered his empty reception room, O'Brien soon came from his office and shook hands with her. The attorney was a short stocky man. His reddish brown hair had receded far back on his splendidly shaped head. Large, brilliant, intelligent gray eyes gleamed from a broad face, which broke into a smile, revealing even, white teeth. He spoke with a brisk cheerfulness, that was welcome to Violet after her encounter with Josiah Conley.

"I must say you've changed quite a lot since the last time I saw you."

His attitude brought a smile to Violet's face, and the tension that had hounded her after the frustrating visit with her grandfather eased considerably. "For the better, I hope."

"Without a doubt." His face sobered. "When I think of how you looked and acted during the six months we kept you when you were a child, I wondered if you would ever be able to overcome the ordeal you had witnessed, but you have, it seems."

"I don't remember anything about the time I spent with my parents, nor of my time here at your house. Actually, my first memory was with Aunt Ruth in Minnesota. I had a sheltered childhood because Aunt Ruth and I were alone so much, and I was an introvert—didn't make friends as much as I should have. I was ashamed that my mother was in prison, and I didn't want my friends to know that. I suppose that's the reason I didn't make many. After I went to college, I became more social."

"Come into my office," he said. "I've canceled all of my appointments today, and have given my secretary the day off. My wife is taking all telephone calls in the house, so we won't be interrupted or overheard. I've guarded your mother's secrets for a long time, and I'll continue to do so unless you decide otherwise. And by the way, Fanny is preparing lunch for you."

"You're being very nice to me."

"My wife and I were both friends of your mother—we went to college together. We have two children of our own, but I've always felt like a father to you. We grew fond of you the few months we kept you before Ruth returned to the States. I want to assist you in every possible way."

"I suppose the first thing I must decide is whether

to allow Mother's story to be aired on that television show.''

''Why are you considering it?''

''To clear her name and memory. If she was innocent, as you've indicated, and if she wouldn't fight for herself, I will do it. Peter Pierce suggested that the story is going to get out anyway, and that I might be better off to have some control over what is told.''

''Frankly, I question if it's wise for you to open up this case. You're going to learn facts that you might be better off not to know.''

''My mother said the same thing, but she also said that if I *had* to know to contact you, for she had buried her past and didn't want to resurrect it. Aunt Ruth would never tell me anything about my father's family—her answer was the same, 'You're better off not to know.' After my introduction to the Conleys yesterday, I've decided she may be right.''

He laughed shortly. ''Yes, I saw you on the late news last night, standing beside the Old Man himself.''

''Are you saying that reception was televised?''

''Of course! Josiah is trying to elect a man to the presidency of the United States, so he can meddle in national political affairs as he's done here in Kansas. He probably had several networks present.''

''Oh, dear, I hope nobody in Maitland saw it.''

''I was watching a local station, but it may have gone nationwide—usually does when a man announces as a presidential candidate.''

''It's too late now for me to worry about my own personal exposure to the media, I suppose, but I didn't have a pleasant time yesterday. I went to his house expecting a short interview with my grandfather, and he wouldn't allow me to leave. When he was busy elsewhere, I slipped out of the house and transferred from the hotel where I'd been staying to another. I only hope that I can get out of town before he learns where I'm staying."

"So you now know the real Josiah Conley—he's domineering. That's why his sons didn't amount to anything, and that grandson, Mike, seems to have suffered the same fate."

"But what about my grandmother, Rachel? Josiah said that she was a wonderful woman, indicating that I looked just like her."

O'Brien nodded. "That's true. I noticed the likeness on television last night, and the resemblance is even more remarkable in person. She *was* a good woman, but I think living with Josiah undoubtedly shortened her life. She's been dead for years."

"When he saw how much I looked like her, he immediately told me that he wanted me to come and live in his home, marry and have children to carry on his name."

"So, now he's decided that you're his granddaughter, has he?"

"What do you mean?" Her violet eyes flashed despairingly as she stared at the lawyer.

"He went to a lot of trouble at your mother's trial to prove that the only reason his son would have abused you or Linda was because you were illegitimate."

Violet gasped. "Surely that isn't true?"

"No, of course not. But you see, as Ryan Conley's daughter, you would have inherited his estate, which was a considerable share of Conley holdings. He had no will, so therefore you would have gotten it. Josiah wasn't about to lose control of a third of his wealth, and somehow he manipulated the court into declaring you illegitimate. There wasn't much emphasis on DNA testing then, and besides, Linda just gave up. She decided that to continue to fight them would make it harder for you, but if she went to prison and out of your life, Ruth could give you a good upbringing.''

''So that's the reason for much of the secrecy—no one wanted me to know that there was a question about my legitimacy.''

''Believe me, there was never any question that you are illegitimate—that was just a falsehood perpetrated by Josiah to serve his ends at the time. Now it's in his interest to recognize you, so last night he introduced you to the world as his granddaughter. But this is one of the sordid questions that may surface if you do authorize the TV program, and be assured that Josiah will fight you all the way.''

''Is he big enough to take on a national television network?''

''He thinks he is.''

Violet stood up and paced the room for a few minutes, stopping to look out the windows where a black-and-white cat walked stealthily across the greening lawn that still sparkled with dew. The telephone rang shrilly, and Violet's pulse raced, but the ringing stopped abruptly as Mrs. O'Brien apparently answered in the house.

''Up until the past six months I lived a fairly peaceful existence, but since last October, I seem to jump from one battleground to another, so I suppose one more fight won't devastate me. I have to know the facts before I can make a judgment on the television show. Where do we start?''

"It will take a couple of days for you to review the material I've accumulated. I have a complete legal portfolio of my trial defense, as well as copies of newspaper reports of the proceedings. I don't do that for all of my court cases, but this situation was such a travesty of justice that I felt constrained to keep a record of everything that happened. You may see any or all of this that you want. But, first, let's go over to the house so you can meet Fanny and have lunch."

Fanny O'Brien was possessed of a lean, energetic body. Whereas William moved with a deliberate step, Fanny seemed in perpetual motion, as if she never stopped to rest. Still, she had a soft manner and her gracious welcome made Violet feel at home. Tears filled her green eyes as she drew Violet into a warm hug.

"My dear, I've prayed often that you would be able to overcome your traumatic past, and it seems that you have." She settled Violet into a comfortable chair, and made no further mention of Violet's reason for being in Kansas City.

While they ate the lunch of cheese-and-broccoli soup, hearty bread, vanilla yogurt and cookies, Fanny and William discussed their family. Violet was invited to view the pictures of their four wonderful grandchildren, and she calculated how many years it would be before Jason and Misty might bear some children. She could become a grandmother before she was thirty—it was an unsettling thought.

They didn't tarry in the house after lunch because O'Brien indicated that it would take several hours to read the court records concerning the trial. As they walked down the long hallway to his office, the lawyer said, "Your father abused your mother physically and emotionally, and as long as he vented his emotions only on her, she submitted. She felt trapped I supposed, as women often do in such circumstances. He also threatened to take you away from her if she ever tried to leave him. She knew that with his wealth, he could do it, too. It was when he also threatened you that she rebelled.''

"This is terrible," Violet moaned as they settled around a table in O'Brien's law library. "My heart has gone out to victims of domestic violence that I've seen in the news, but I can hardly stand to believe that my mother and I were treated in such a manner."

"As I understand he never actually hurt you until the night Linda shot him, but he kept a loaded gun handy and sometimes threatened both of you with it. That fatal night, he picked you up and appeared about to hurt you. She grabbed the gun and pleaded with him to leave you alone. They struggled and when the gun went off by accident, he was shot."

Violet sighed deeply, unable to speak. "I'm glad I was too young to remember it," she said finally.

"I did the best I could at the trial, proving that she acted in self-defense, but I'll have to admit that Josiah Conley outmaneuvered me. He had a bevy of high-powered lawyers, and I just couldn't compete with them. And when Linda wouldn't even testify in her own defense, I just couldn't get her acquitted."

All of her life Violet had wondered why her mother hadn't loved her, but the more she heard, the more she realized that Linda's every action of the past was motivated by overwhelming love for her daughter. Why did her mother have to die before Violet realized the extent of that love?

After four hours of reading the court proceedings,

Violet knew the whole story—how her mother had been portrayed as a woman of questionable character, even mentally unstable, and her father shown to be an admirable man, perhaps even defending himself from a violent wife.

The trial had indeed been a travesty of justice, but did she want all of this aired to the nation on Peter Pierce's show? She dropped her head to her hands when she laid aside the last paper.

Her voice muffled in her hands, she said, "Everyone was right. I shouldn't have delved into the past. Now, I'll have to live with the knowledge that I had a beast for a father, and that my grandfather conspired to send my mother to prison."

"Linda said that Ryan wasn't difficult at first, but when they came to live here in Kansas City, he began to drink heavily and their marriage became a disaster."

Compassionately, O'Brien said, "Why not stay with us tonight? You will need to come tomorrow and read the newspapers anyway. We would be pleased to have you. I don't like for you to be alone."

"Thank you, but if you'll telephone for a taxi, I'll go back to the hotel. I know how to find your office now—I'll drive out tomorrow."

Violet did appreciate O'Brien's offer, but all she wanted now was Roger. She had to telephone him as soon as she could, to hear his kind voice, and know, by the soft inflection of his words, that he loved her—even over the phone, Roger's voice conveyed a caress.

She hurriedly dialed his number as soon as she reached her hotel room. Jason answered, saying his father hadn't come home yet. So she waited almost an hour, with her hand on the phone, before he finally called.

"Oh, Roger, it's good to talk to you."

"You sound upset," he said. "Are you all right?"

"No—I've had a terrible day finding out about my father's death and my mother's trial. And after that day with my grandfather yesterday, I've about had it."

"Have you made up your mind about what you intend to do about all these new developments?"

"No, I'm too upset to even think. Roger..." she paused, tapping her fingers on the table. "Roger, I probably shouldn't even ask this, but could you come here? If you will come by plane, I'll pay for the ticket. I know I shouldn't unload all of my troubles on you, but I just don't know what to do. If you could be with me when I give my grandfather an answer, and if you could talk to Mr. O'Brien, it would be such a help to me."

There was a long silence, and Violet held her breath. Surely he wouldn't refuse when she needed him so desperately.

"I'm sorry, Violet. You're on your own with this one. It's one situation where you must make decisions without me. There's a lot at stake for you, and I don't want to sway your judgment with my opinions. I won't come, but I'll support any decision you make. I hope you understand."

"I understand perfectly," Violet said, biting her lips to control her voice. "I'm sorry I asked you. Goodbye." When she replaced the receiver, Violet felt as if she had cut the lifeline on her last vestige of hope. After he had promised that he would always be available when she needed him, Roger had failed her. She couldn't believe she had heard him correctly, and she

kept thinking he would return her call to say he would
come to her after all, but the phone didn't ring.

Violet undressed and lay upon the bed, although she
didn't expect to sleep. Once she thought of telephon-
ing Pastor Tom, but what could he do for her now?
As she stared dry-eyed at the ceiling, Violet remembered Jesus's words from the cross, "My God, My
God, why have you forsaken me?" It must have been
an anguished cry for already his friends had betrayed,
denied and deserted him, but the ultimate despair came
at that moment when He feared that God, too, had
deserted Him.

Strangely enough, even though Roger had repudiated her, she didn't feel forsaken by God, and it gave
her the strength to go on. She didn't want to return to
Maitland, didn't think she could possibly face Roger,
but what else could she do? Her home and her job
were there, as were her friends. She could eventually
go back to Minnesota and live near Aunt Ruth, who
would be glad to have her, and that might be a good
move.

For the time being, at least, she would have to return
to Maitland to make the decisions that loomed
ahead—how to evade her grandfather's clutches and
whether or not to approve the documentary on her
mother's trial. Roger wouldn't help her make those
decisions, but her faith was strong that God would.
God had never said that his followers would be exempt
from problems, although He promised His presence in
the midst of trouble.

She thought of the many times in the Bible when
He had brought others from the depth of despair and
made them viable people again. Probably David was
one of the best biblical examples to prove that God's

people were not exempt from trouble. Although expressly chosen by God to lead the Hebrew nation, his father-in-law had plotted his death, his sons had disappointed him, one had even aspired to usurp his father and the Hebrew king lost some of his sons by death. Yet David had praised God even in the midst of his trials. She remembered his words, "Why are you downcast, O my soul? Why so disturbed within me? Put your hope in God, for I will yet praise him, my Savior and my God."

Those words described Violet's condition. Her soul was disturbed, but today's happenings had brought her to the place where she recognized that her only hope was in God. Roger was human, so it was natural that he would disappoint and fail her. Larry had hurt her by his rejection. Her mother and father had left her a nasty, devastating and scandalous heritage. Only God had the power to sustain her. And although she knew some momentous decisions awaited her on the morrow, her heart was at peace and she was able to sleep when she remembered other words of the Psalmist, believing that what God had done for David, He would do for her: "I lie down and sleep; I wake again, because the Lord sustains me."

After she showered and dressed the next morning, Violet went downstairs to the restaurant for breakfast. Although she hadn't eaten since her lunch with the O'Briens yesterday, she had little appetite, but she ordered coffee, toast and oatmeal. She didn't believe today's revelations could possibly be worse than what she had endured yesterday, but whatever she faced, she knew better than to tackle it on an empty stomach.

As she walked across the lobby after eating, the clerk called, "You had a telephone call while you were out of your room. I didn't know you were in the restaurant or I could have paged you." He handed her a sheet of paper, on which he had written, "Return the call of Josiah Conley."

So he had traced her. She should has suspected that.

Coming to a quick decision, she said to the clerk, "I'll be checking out of the hotel this morning. I had intended to stay until tomorrow, but I believe I can finish my work and leave today."

She hurriedly packed her bags. Now that her grandfather had found out where she was, he might very well come to the hotel when she didn't return his call. She absolutely couldn't talk to the man until she had time to assimilate what she had learned in the past few days. If she approved the documentary on her mother's trial, her grandfather would be very unhappy, and she had decided that she must think and pray more before she came to a decision. As soon as she finished with O'Brien, she would head toward Maitland. Today was Friday, and she could be home by Saturday evening, which would give her some time of preparation before returning to school on Monday.

"Has something else happened?" O'Brien asked immediately upon seeing Violet, and she surmised that her demeanor must appear even worse than yesterday.

"Well, yes, you could say that," she said bitterly. "I telephoned my fiancé last night, and he was reluctant to talk to me. When I asked him to come here to talk with you about the trial, and to go with me to talk with my grandfather, he told me I would have to handle this one by myself."

Violet paused, and her thoughts were bitter, but she was tearless and resigned to doing without Roger. She really couldn't blame him for turning her down; she had burdened him with her problems so much the past few months. Perhaps he thought it was time for her to act more independently. But that still didn't prevent her from feeling dejected.

"He probably knows more about Josiah Conley than you do."

"Quite possibly, for I didn't know anything until Tuesday. Then this morning, I had a telephone call from my grandfather at the hotel, but I wasn't in my room to receive the call. I'd changed hotels to prevent his tracing me, but he did. As soon as I finish here, I'm leaving town. I can't encounter him again. I'm afraid of him."

"And so you should be. Very few people have ever confronted Josiah Conley and come out the victor. I hope you don't think I'm just prejudiced against the man. I have proof of my allegations. He has a thirst for power, and whom he can't control, he destroys."

"So does that mean he will destroy me if I don't do what he wants?"

"Perhaps, but if you do what he wants, you'll also be destroyed. You have a better chance of survival if you stay away from him. It's too bad you had the misfortune to have Josiah Conley for your grandfather."

"I've wondered why my mother ever married into the Conley family. Surely, she must have known what they were like."

"Remember, she didn't live in Kansas City. She met your father in Topeka, where he was managing a branch of Midwest Enterprises. He was a handsome man, with a lot of charisma, and she didn't consider his family when she fell in love with him. I believe

Ryan wanted her because she was mild-tempered and went along with everything he wanted. He'd had enough domination all of his life, and Linda's quiet ways salved his ego. They were happy, at first, until Josiah called them back to Kansas City—that's when the trouble started.''

"I'll spend the morning reading old newspapers, and then I'm going home, although I suppose I won't even be safe there."

"Didn't you say your fiancé is a policeman? He can protect you."

Violet grimaced. "Don't forget, he may not want to be my fiancé now?"

She didn't learn much more from the newspapers than she already knew, and by early afternoon, O'Brien took her into his private office for a consultation. His secretary was working today, and their conversations were guarded.

"So now you know," he said.

"Yes, and I'm not sure I'm any better off, but I do know. Now what do I do with my knowledge?"

"That is your decision."

"You don't know how weary I've become of hearing those words the past few months," Violet said. "Decisions! Decisions!"

"But consider—have they been good decisions?"

She thought of the decisions she had made. She had defied Larry to assure that Janie received the Best of Show award. That was good. She had decided to bring her mother from prison, and that, too, had turned out well. She had become engaged to Roger, and that was the best decision of all, or at least it seemed that way until their telephone conversation last night.

"Up until I made the decision to meet my grandfather and check into my mother's past—they were good. But I disregarded the advice of my mother and Aunt Ruth. Only time will tell whether that was a good or bad decision. Right now, it doesn't seem good.''

''Go back to Maitland before you come to any conclusion. Think it over carefully, and if I can be of any help to you, I'm as close as the telephone.''

Violet left Kansas City by late evening, and breathed a sigh of relief when she accessed I-70, crossed the border into Missouri, and glimpsed the beautiful skyline of the city in her rearview mirror. As long as she was in Kansas, she didn't feel safe from her grandfather's clutches. Her progress on Saturday was impeded when a freak spring snowstorm swept through central Missouri. By late evening, the sun was out, melting the snow, but the treacherous roads had delayed Violet, necessitating a stopover in a motel, and she arrived in Maitland shortly after noon on Sunday.

Chapter Nine

When Violet parked in her driveway, she leaned her head on the steering wheel and breathed a prayer of thanksgiving. It had been a frustrating journey, for at times, she was hardly conscious of where she was and what she was doing. Surely God must have given her special attention on the long drive home, because in her present mental state of mind, she didn't believe she was capable of driving an automobile.

After she put Kansas City behind her, she had pushed the threat of her grandfather in the background, but even then she couldn't concentrate on operating the auto. Over and over she wondered how to effect a reconciliation with Roger, or if she should even try, but now that she was back in Maitland, she had an overpowering desire to see him. All her life, she had been alone, but she had gotten accustomed to Roger's company and care, and she was completely bereft without him. But if he no longer wanted her? She could barely stand the thought. She admitted that she couldn't blame any man for not wanting to marry a person with a family background such as hers. But that hadn't seemed to matter to Roger. Perhaps she was reading something into his refusal to come to Kansas City that he hadn't intended. Was it fair to deny him the opportunity to defend himself?

Again she had no control over her actions as she went immediately to the phone and dialed Roger's number. Misty answered, and when Violet asked for Roger she said, "He isn't here, Miss Conley. Right after lunch, he put the dogs in the truck, and I suppose he went to the farm."

After thanking Misty, Violet changed into rugged clothing and headed out of town. Mentally and physically, she was exhausted, but she would never rest until she saw Roger, believing she would be able to tell from his facial expression if he was through with her.

She parked her car beside his house and walked up the farm road toward the hillock. An hour later, she was sitting on the tailgate of the truck when he came out of the trees followed by the two dogs, who set up a howl when they saw her.

Did his steps decelerate as if he were reluctant to meet her? She couldn't be sure, and she didn't speak when he came to the truck. He went through the regular ritual of giving the animals food and drink before he came to stand beside her.

"When did you get back?" he asked.

"About noon." She looked at him piercingly. "I wondered if I should return at all."

He playfully chucked her under the chin, but his dark eyes were watchful as he said, "Did becoming a rich woman sound better than anything you could find in Maitland?"

Tears welled in her eyes. "Roger, do you think any amount of money would make up for losing you? Why have you been so cold and distant with me this week? I thought if there was any person in this whole world I could depend upon to understand what I've endured the past few days, it was you." Her lower lip quivered, and she clamped it between her teeth to stop the trembling, but she couldn't do anything about the tears that cascaded down her cheeks.

"But I haven't been…" Roger began, as he moved closer and stood eye level with her as she sat on the truck.

"Yes, you have. You told me once you would be there for me any time I needed you, and I've never needed support as much as I have this past week, and you wouldn't even let me talk to you about it."

Her tears turned into sobs, and Roger gathered her into his arms. "Oh, my dear, you have it all wrong. I was trying to do what was best for you—I didn't mean to hurt you." He rocked her back and forth in his embrace, and her body shook as her sobs faded into the plaintive cries of a wounded animal. Roger was crying, too, and he couldn't speak, but finally he swiped his eyes with the back of his hand and cleared his throat noisily.

"Come, sweetheart, let's drive down to the house. You're cold, and we need to clear up this misunderstanding between us." He lifted her from the seat and carried her to the truck cab. He soon secured the dogs, and they drove in silence to the house.

"Are you hungry?" he asked, as he opened the door into his retreat.

"Probably. I haven't eaten anything today. I may not have eaten yesterday—I don't remember."

He turned on the heater. "Let me take your coat," Roger said. "The room will heat in a hurry. We'll eat later, but let's talk first."

They sat on the couch, and Roger pulled her close, for Violet was still shaking, and she didn't know if the trembling was caused from cold or stress.

"You couldn't have felt more lonely than I have this week," he said. "When you telephoned Tuesday night and said your grandfather wanted to make you his heir, and that he would accept me sight unseen as your husband, and all it would cost me was to change my name to Conley, I thought that was funny, at first. Then, I flipped on the late news and saw the telecast where you were at your grandfather's palatial home, wearing that fancy black dress and sporting diamonds that I couldn't buy with ten years' salary, seemingly right at home in that environment. Talk about feeling alone! I didn't sleep at all that night, afraid of losing you, saddened by how this turn of events could ruin our lives."

"But I told you—I was virtually forced to stay for that reception and dressed up like a mannequin by his servant. My grandfather is a man who will not take no for an answer. He practically imprisoned me."

"Well, he will have to take no from me. I couldn't possibly be happy as your husband if I succumbed to the lure of riches, changed my name to Conley and became a tool of your grandfather's. But on the other hand, I didn't think I had the right to deny you your rightful inheritance, and if you wanted to take him up on his proposal, I wouldn't stand in your way. I would sacrifice my happiness for yours."

Violet pushed out of his arms, and her vivid eyes blazed in anger. "I wish people would stop being so self-sacrificial for me. My mother denied me for years because she was doing what was best for me, and I grew up without knowing my mother. And you plunged me to the depth of despair when you told me I was on my own 'with this one.' Did you consider that I didn't believe I should reject my grandfather's proposal without discussing it with you? We're engaged to be married—I thought from now on, we didn't make independent decisions.''

Roger chuckled, kissed her lightly on the lips and hugged her close again.

''I hadn't thought of that.''

''Not many men would turn down a chance to become a millionaire overnight. You've admitted that it won't be easy for you to put two children through college and take on a new family besides. If you were willing to work for my grandfather, why should I say no for you?''

He smoothed back her hair and kissed her forehead. ''I'll admit that I was tempted for a while. My parents were poor, and my mother needs everything she has for her own livelihood—I will never inherit anything from her. What I have, I've worked for, and when the going has been rough, I've often wondered how it would be to never have to worry about where my next dollar would come from. But I've heard of Josiah Conley, and although I hadn't connected him with you, he has the reputation of being a hard man—he wouldn't give us everything he has without expecting a lot in return. I don't believe we could have a happy marriage living in his household.''

''Neither do I. That day I went to his house, I felt like a prisoner. He was determined that I was going to stay there, and I had to slip out of the house when he was busy elsewhere to even return to my hotel. I changed hotels, and he found me there, but I left Kansas City without returning his calls, for when I found out how he had manipulated my mother's trial, I knew there was no place for him in my life. That's why I telephoned you—I hoped you would come to me as you had when Mother died, go with me to tell my grandfather we were rejecting his offer, and drive home with me. I knew he wouldn't accept my refusal if I didn't have your support, but when you were so unapproachable, I wouldn't insist.''

Roger pulled her close. He kissed her closed eyelids, her throbbing throat, the tips of her ears, and each finger. When he came to her lips, the dull heartache that Violet had endured for the past few days disappeared, and she laced her arms behind his neck, cherishing the warmth and strength of his embrace. The agony of the past week receded, and his caresses brought assurance of a future that she was eager to start.

"Let me promise you something now," Roger whispered, his lips nuzzling the soft curve of her throat. "I'll never forsake you again—no matter what you face, I'll be there. Any decisions we make from now on, we'll make them together. This vow is just as sacred to me as the one I'll take on our wedding day when I promise to love you 'until death do us part.'"

When he ended their embrace, Violet said, "Then it seems we've agreed that we have no interest in accepting my grandfather's proposal, but we have to make a decision on that documentary about my mother and father. And don't tell me that I'm on 'my own' with it. It's a sordid story, and we may not want our

children to have to live with its aftermath if we make
the facts widespread.''

''I want to hear about what you learned from the
lawyer, but if you haven't had any food today, we
must find a restaurant. I have snack food in this house,
but nothing substantial. I'll leave the truck here, and
we can go in your car to a restaurant in a nearby
town.''

''I do feel hungry, but I don't want to eat in Maitland.'' She ran her fingers over her hair and touched
her hot, swollen face. ''I must look terrible.''

Roger kissed the tip of her red, sniffy nose. ''Not
to me. You look wonderful, especially when I've been
living with the fear that I'd lost you.''

''I dread going back to school tomorrow, but I'll
have to make some preparations tonight, so after
we've eaten, I'll go home and work. Perhaps we can
be together tomorrow night.''

''I go on night shift in a few hours for a week, but
I can see you early tomorrow evening.''

On their way to the restaurant, Violet told Roger
briefly about the death of Ryan Conley by her
mother's hand, and they agreed that in the interest of
justice the facts of the trial should be aired on television.

When the phone rang right before bedtime, Violet
assumed it was Roger checking in to see how she felt,
but to her surprise, Olivia Holland was on the phone.

''I hoped that I would catch you at home,'' Mrs.
Holland said in the cultivated, honey tones she used
when she wanted to be the most pleasing. ''Larry said
you were due back for school in the morning.''

''Yes, I came home about noon today.''

There was a pause, which Mrs. Holland finally broke. "I was pleased to learn that you *are* related to the Kansas City Conleys. I met your grandparents several years ago at a political rally in Saint Louis. I hope you will remember me to them the next time you see them."

Apparently Roger wasn't the only Maitland resident to see her in the splendor of the Conley mansion.

"My grandmother died a few years ago, and I doubt that I will be going there again. I went to Kansas City for another purpose, but my grandfather had asked to see me, so I did pay him a visit, but I had little in common with him, so we won't be developing a filial relationship."

"But, Violet, if you'll forgive me for advising you, if Josiah Conley wants to recognize you, it would be well for you to accept his patronage. He's a big man in that region, and he could do much for you."

Yes, he could make me a prisoner to his will and plans, Violet thought, but she let Mrs. Holland ramble on.

"I appreciate your concern, Mrs. Holland, but this is a matter I will have to work out with my grandfather."

Before Mrs. Holland terminated the conversation, Violet was half tempted to tell her that Josiah Conley would make her his heir if she would come to live with him, marry and have a family to carry on the family fortune. Mrs. Holland would probably rouse Larry out of his easy chair and send him over to propose immediately, but she resisted the temptation. Violet didn't intend to circulate the fact that she'd had a multimillion-dollar legacy laid at her feet and that she was going to reject it.

*   *   *

Monday was a hectic time for Violet. The first day back after a long break was always a difficult time to corral the students into working, but after three years of teaching, Violet expected that. What she did not expect was all the attention she received because of the reception she had attended at the Conley mansion in Kansas City. Everyone in Maitland must know by now about her connection to the Czar of the Midwest, as she had learned Josiah Conley was often called.

She hadn't been in her room ten minutes when Larry stopped in, all smiles. He put his arm around her shoulders, and she cringed at his touch.

"It's good to see you this morning, Violet. All ready for the avalanche of students?"

She moved away from his embrace as she continued to place worksheets on the students' desks. She glanced at the clock. "I'd better be ready in twenty minutes, but it's always hard for me to be enthusiastic after a holiday and therefore it's difficult to motivate the students."

"I would think that the terrific week you had would have given you lots of motivation. Why didn't you tell me you were related to the Kansas City Conleys?"

"I didn't know it myself until two months ago. I told you that I didn't know anything about my father's people." She stopped working long enough to give him a piercing glance.

He was toying with a paperweight on her desk and wouldn't meet her gaze. "It doesn't make any difference to me."

"A few months ago I was convinced that my questionable heritage was vastly important to you."

The hall barriers had been removed, and students

were entering the halls, laughing and shouting, happy to see their peers after the break. Larry started toward the door. "May I take you to dinner one night this week?"

"No, thank you, Larry. I suppose you should know that Roger Gibson and I are engaged—we plan to be married in June."

He stopped abruptly. "Marry Roger Gibson? You told me he was nothing to you but a friend."

"Yes, and I was as surprised as you are to learn that, while he *is* my best friend, he's also the man I love and want to marry."

"I suppose *he* knew that you are Josiah Conley's granddaughter."

"As a matter of fact, he does know, but he asked me to marry him before he knew it. What are you suggesting?"

"I'm suggesting nothing—just figure it out for yourself."

Angrily, Violet said, "Don't judge other people's actions by your own, Larry."

Violet lost count of how many pupils mentioned seeing her on television, and several of the girls made comments, such as, "Gee, it didn't even look like you, Miss Conley, with all of those diamonds and that sleek dress. Did you enjoy that big party?"

Misty sidled up to her and said quietly, with a touch of Roger's humor, "I didn't know my new mama was a society lady."

"She isn't," Violet replied. "That was a once-in-a-lifetime experience. You'll have to put up with the same old Violet Conley you've always known."

With a slight grin, Misty said, "That suits me."

Before the closing bell rang, Violet rued the day she

was born a Conley. When Nan came in after the closing bell, Violet said, "How fickle can people be? Where are our values? When my mother's prison record became known, people turned against me. When they learn that I have a rich grandfather, although he is a scoundrel, and by some accounts, *should* be in prison, I've become the most popular person on the staff. Where are our values?" she repeated.

"Face it! Generally speaking, people are materialistic, and we're judged not by what we are, but by what we have."

"I don't have any more now than I did six months ago, and never will inherit any of the Conley millions. The cost is too great."

Nan laughed. "When you come into a fortune, don't forget who your true friends were when you were poor."

"Cut it out, Nan. I've had about all I can take today. I don't enjoy being in the limelight."

"As I told you when there was such a furor over your mother, this will all die down when something else unusual happens to excite the populace. Maitland is a nice place to live, but it is a *small* town, and no one can have any secrets. If you lived in a large city, your debut into society would hardly have been noticed."

"I'm worried that all of this publicity might come between Roger and me."

They walked out of the school together, and Nan reassured, "You don't have anything to worry about. Roger has a level head on his shoulders."

At home, she had two calls on her answering machine. One was from Josiah Conley's secretary, which she erased without answering. The other was from Peter Pierce. He hadn't wasted any time, she thought wryly.

She returned his call, and when he answered the phone, she identified herself and said, "I've decided to authorize the documentary on the episode between my mother and father. You will have to contact my attorney for details and also for any financial arrangements. I think you met William O'Brien when you were previously in Kansas City."

After she completed that call, Violet telephoned O'Brien.

"Right or wrong," she said as soon as the attorney answered the phone, "I've authorized Peter Pierce to air the story of my parents' problems. I hope you will act for me in deciding what information to release and also the financial arrangements. He had told me that he would pay $500,000 for publishing rights, and if you don't think that is enough, see that he pays what is just. Whatever the proceeds, I want you to set up the amount in a Linda Conley Foundation to provide college scholarships for deserving girls who couldn't further their education in any other way."

"I'll be happy to act for you in the matter, but I'll telephone you with the details before any papers are signed. And what about the bank account that your mother had—shall I transfer that to you now?"

"Yes. I'll use that money, rather than put it in the foundation, for I have her funeral expenses to pay, and I do plan to marry soon. I believe that is the way Mother would want it. She earned that money, and I'm not hesitant to use it, but I don't want to profit from the documentary, to prove to myself, if to no one else, that my motives weren't mercenary."

"Just a word of warning, Violet. You'll not be able

to avoid Josiah Conley. The man is determined to get what he wants, and he will use every force at his command to bend you to his will. He wants you to raise up a dynasty for him, but he's not above casting you aside as soon as you provide him with a grandson or two."

"Isn't there anything good about him? I refuse to believe that there isn't *something* worthwhile in everybody."

"I'll admit I'm biased against him, but I see nothing in him to admire."

"Despite all I'd heard about him, I couldn't help but like the man. He can be charming if he wants to be."

"So can any scoundrel! Be careful in any dealings with him."

"I've been wondering if I shouldn't notify him by mail that I'm not interested in accepting his proposition. As my attorney, will you write to him and tell him my decision?"

"With pleasure," O'Brien assured her. "I'll mail you a copy."

"Please be kind about it. I don't want to antagonize him any more than I have to."

After her conversation with O'Brien, Violet had little appetite, but she placed a chicken breast in the broiler, and while it cooked, she prepared a salad and toasted a slice of sourdough bread. During her meal, she looked out the dining room window and marveled at how the foliage in her backyard had changed in the week she had been gone. Daffodils and tulips created an aura of yellow, red and pink hues. The forsythia's yellow blooms swayed gently in the southwest breeze. For beauty, her yard certainly came off second best when compared with the floral display at the Conley mansion, but she liked this one better.

When the kitchen was tidied, Violet took a cup of tea and went to the living room. She felt spiritually drained, and she picked up the Bible before she settled into her lounge chair. She was troubled about her own personality, and what she had to offer Roger. She pondered the age-old question of the greatest determinant in molding character—heredity or environment? Had she inherited any of the abominable traits of the Conleys? What of her father's temper or her grandfather's domineering attitude—did she have the same flaw in her character, lurking somewhere beneath the surface waiting to assert itself? Could she hope that if she inherited anything from the Conleys that it might be from her grandmother?

The future seemed bleak when she dwelt on these possibilities, but as she riffled the pages of the Bible in her lap, she knew without a doubt that, like her mother, she was hesitant to cause conflict. She dreaded the thought of being involved in a confrontation with her grandfather that was bound to come when he learned about the documentary, but she wasn't as troubled as she might have been a few months ago. God had provided the guidance and support she needed to bring her mother into her home, to cope with Linda's death, to accept her father's faulty character and the terrible circumstances that led to his death by his wife's hand, and the disappointment and loss she felt when Roger had forsaken her. These were not situations that Violet would ever want to experience again, but as she looked back on them, she knew that each crisis and its resolution had increased her faith in God and her realization that nothing she encountered in the future would remove her beyond the realm of His care. It was a comforting thought.

She opened the Bible to the Psalms. What a blessing that, years before the birth of Christ, these inspired writers had been able to put into words the path that a Christian should follow. Violet looked down at Psalm 73 on the printed page before her and received encouragement from the revelation God had given to the psalmist: "Yet I am always with you; you hold me by my right hand. You guide me with your counsel, and afterward you will take me into glory. Whom have I in heaven but you? And being with you, I desire nothing on earth. My flesh and my heart may fail, but God is the strength of my heart and my portion forever."

Violet sensed that she couldn't avoid an unpleasant confrontation with Josiah P. Conley, but with God's help, she would know what to do, relying on Him for the guidance she needed. The comfort of God's presence overwhelmed her, and she was at peace from the day's frustrations. Violet was napping when Roger knocked, and she yawned when she opened the door.

"What a welcome!" Roger said, laughing. "I expected you to greet me with open arms, and all I get is a yawn."

"I had just dropped off to sleep," Violet excused herself. She spread out her arms. "But the arms are always open. Come on in." She gave him a tight hug and picked up the teacup on the table. "I'll make some fresh tea. That will awaken me. How was your day?"

"Frustrating!"

"Oh-oh! So was mine—we may come to loggerheads before the evening is over."

He leaned on the snack bar while they waited for

the water to boil. She dropped two tea bags into the teapot. "What made yours so frustrating?" Roger asked.

With a side glance at him, Violet said, "The staff and students at Maitland High are favorably impressed that I'm the granddaughter of Josiah B. Conley. My status has risen considerably. I was the most popular person on campus today."

"And you found that displeasing?" he said, toying with a dish mat on the counter.

"Very much so. It particularly rankled when my principal asked me for a date this week. How could he have had the nerve?"

"I assume you turned him down."

"Of course. My heart is already spoken for. I thought you knew that."

"I suspected it." He smiled at her and picked up the tray she had prepared and carried it to the living room. She sat on the couch, and he handed her a cup of tea and pulled up a footstool close to her.

"But as for Larry approaching you, his mother is probably pressuring him. If Olivia Holland can see any possibility of getting her hands on any of the Conley millions, she won't pass it up."

"That's my opinion, too. I do think Larry is fond of me, but he does dance to his mother's tune. She telephoned me last night and was all sweetness and charm. I didn't bother to disillusion her by telling her the complete state of affairs between Josiah Conley and me, for I didn't consider it any of her business." She sipped on the tea, hesitating. "I told Larry that I planned to marry you in two months, and he was certainly annoyed, even to the extent of suggesting that your interest in me was influenced by my possible inheritance. Perhaps I shouldn't have told you that, but if you should hear it, I didn't want you to think I believed it."

Roger grimaced, causing the etched lines on his face to deepen. "Some of my acquaintances made similar remarks today. That's one reason for *my* frustration."

"Larry's remark really upset me, for I feared that if you heard such a rumor it would scare you off again."

He reached for her hand and lifted it to his lips. "Violet, I've made a vow to you. I'm in for the long haul—the only way I'll leave you now is if you chase me away."

Her fingers tightened around his strong hand. "That isn't likely."

When she started to tell him in detail what she had learned about her mother and father in Kansas City, Roger moved to the couch beside her, and with one arm around her shoulder, he took her hand. As the circumstances of her father's death unfolded, Roger murmured compassionately more than once, and often used his handkerchief to blot the tears from Violet's eyes.

When she concluded, she said, "It's a sordid tale, but I've agreed to allow the program to be aired and have authorized my attorney in Kansas City to make the necessary negotiations."

"Do you know how long before the program will be on television?"

"I have no idea, but Peter Pierce will want to present it as soon as possible, I should think, to be ahead of some other journalist who might not ask for permission."

"Josiah Conley won't be pleased."

"I know! Mr. O'Brien has warned me that he won't give up on his desire to have me move into his household and mother a dynasty for him, and that I should be aware of possible underhanded tactics."

"I know Conley by reputation only, but he's reported to be the kind of man who might exert pressure to have both of us lose our jobs so he could force us to do his bidding."

"Does he has that much influence in Illinois?"

"I don't think so, but if he should hook up with the Holland faction, we can expect anything." He paused, and a whimsical expression crossed his face. "Violet, are you sure you really want to marry me? If you consider that Olivia Holland would welcome you gladly if you should effect a reconciliation with your grandfather, you're actually turning down two fortunes to marry me, and I'll never be able to provide you with anything more than a moderate living. Violet, are you sure?"

Violet gazed for a long moment into Roger's deep brown eyes, and in a flash, her mind monitored all of the characteristics that had drawn her to him. He was a responsible father. He was respected in the community for his forcefulness as a law officer, and also for his compassion for those who were involved in crime. He had a sense of humor. His everyday living exemplified the tenets of his Christian beliefs. Violet's hand lifted to caress Roger's face, and the quick response in his eyes to her touch fortified her assurance that with this man she would find a marriage that would satisfy her physical and emotional needs as well as guarantee a secure and harmonious future. She kissed her fingers and rubbed them tenderly across his lips.

"Riches can't provide what I want in a husband. Believe me, I've stopped looking back to the past. I want you. Are you trying to squirm out of marrying me?" she asked with a twinkle in her eye.

"No, but I wanted to give you one last opportunity to back out before I gave you this." He pulled a jeweler's box from his pocket. He removed a diamond ring and placed it on the third finger of her left hand. "Are you willing to accept this ring, remembering that you have to take me in the bargain?"

Violet caught her breath and held it momentarily as she looked down at the cluster of small diamonds, which probably didn't total a carat, but even at that, was more expensive than Roger may have been able to afford. For a fleeting moment, she compared it to the ornate, multidiamonded ring that Josiah had made her wear at the reception, and it was an unfavorable comparison on the part of the Conley heirloom. The small ring that Roger offered her spelled freedom— freedom to be her own person, freedom to love Roger and rear their children as they wanted, freedom to worship God and to serve Him in the environment of a Christian home. On the other hand, she envisioned the expensive Conley ring as a collar that would enslave her and make her a bondwoman to her grandfather's whims. Her decision didn't take a second thought.

"I want to marry you now," she said, "but I suppose we should hold to our original plans. At least, let's announce it in the paper, so everyone will be aware."

He kissed her as she moved closer into the shelter of his arms. She perceived that their life's journey would not be without its problems and frustrations, but in Roger she had found the support she needed to weather the storms.

"Why not? There isn't any need to keep our engagement secret. After all, we're being married in two months."

Chapter Ten

The telephone was ringing when Violet entered the kitchen, her arms filled with two bags of groceries. She hurriedly deposited the bags on the sink counter and snatched the receiver just before the answering machine took over.

"My name is Clifford Skeen. I'm trying to contact a Violet Conley, who is the teacher of Janie Skeen."

"This is Violet Conley, and Janie Skeen is a pupil in one of my classes."

"My wife and I are in Maitland, and if you have time, we would like to stop by for a short visit with you to get some information about Janie. I understand you're a friend of hers."

"Please do, I'd like very much to see you," Violet said and gave him directions to her house from the motel where he was staying. Violet's heart was alternately pounding and singing as she hurriedly stored the groceries in the proper places. Could this be the answer to Janie's future? She picked up newspapers and other items from the living room. Saturday was not only grocery day, but cleaning day as well, and she sometimes became careless in her housekeeping near the end of the week.

She was watching at the window when the white sedan drove into her driveway. A tall, lanky man with a full black beard came around the car and opened the passenger side door for his wife. When they entered the house, Clifford Skeen shook hands with Violet.

"Miss Conley, this is my wife, Alta."

Alta Skeen, who appeared to be at least ten years younger than her husband, was not a beautiful woman, but she had dark green expressive eyes that impressed Violet with their wisdom and kindness. She stood shoulder to shoulder with her tall husband, and although she exhibited a quiet manner, Violet wondered if Alta was not the driving force in their marriage, if it was she who had made this union more successful than the one Clifford Skeen had apparently had with his first wife.

When they were seated in the living room, Skeen cleared his throat. "Miss Conley," he said, "I'll come to the point of my visit. I have reason to believe that Janie Skeen is my daughter."

Violet smiled. "I hope that you are. Janie needs a real family."

"Where is Janie's mother?"

"She doesn't have any idea. It seems her mother disappeared, and when the state social agency couldn't find her, they placed Janie in a foster home."

Clifford Skeen shook his head in disgust. "To think that a child of mine would have to live under such conditions. If her mother didn't want the child, there are a half dozen people in our respective families who would have wanted her. I didn't remarry for several years, so I couldn't have cared for her, but my mother would have taken her gladly.''

Alta spoke for the first time. "You see, Miss Conley, we aren't able to have a child, although it's important to both of us. We were applying to adopt when we heard from a sister of Clifford's first wife that he had a child. We had a younger child in mind, but we decided that if Janie was Clifford's child, we wanted to give her a good home if she needed one. Clifford wanted to have a relationship with her no matter what. We finally traced her here, to Maitland.''

"My first wife's family is very similar to mine—small-town folks," Clifford said. "As far as I know, Janie's mother is the only one that doesn't live a respectable life. When we were married, I didn't know that Pat had a problem with alcohol, and I tried to help her overcome it, but she couldn't seem to. She left me, and after two years when she didn't return, I got a divorce on the basis of desertion, but I had no idea there was a child. Alta and I have talked it over since then and prayed for guidance, and we want to take her, if we can be convinced that she is my daughter.''

Briefly Violet explained about Janie's flight from her mother, how she had lived on the streets for six months before she had been found and brought to Maitland.

"Do you know when she was born?" Skeen asked.

"I can check the exact date on the school records, but I believe that she was born on May 26, sixteen years ago.''

Clifford thought for a few moments. "Then she could be my daughter, for it was about six months before that when my wife deserted me, so we were still living together when Janie was conceived. All things considered, I suppose I would prefer that she take a DNA test to prove that I am her biological father. Do you think she would submit to such a test? Do you think Janie would want to live with us?''

''Janie is the only one who can answer those questions, although I do know she wants the security of a home. She's content with Mrs. Grady, but she worries about having to leave there and go to another foster mother.''

''Would you talk to Janie for us? Or perhaps you could invite her over here and we could talk to her now.''

''Nothing would please me more than to have you take Janie, but I wonder if you shouldn't move in a different direction. She's a ward of the state right now, and I believe you should work through the agency that handles her case. If her mother is still living, that will complicate the situation. Perhaps you should hire a lawyer to contact them for you.''

''Yes,'' Alta agreed, ''I can see that is the best procedure, for if we don't handle this legally and wisely, we could ruin our chances to take Janie into our home, but I would like to see her. We are both overanxious, I suppose,'' she admitted with a smile. ''I think I was born to be a mother, and I've often wondered why God hasn't sent us a child. When I learned about Janie, I hoped that He had withheld a baby from us so that we would be ready to take Clifford's daughter.''

Hearing these words from Alta encouraged Violet, because after the spiritual climate Janie had enjoyed in Mrs. Grady's home, it would have been difficult to see her thrust into a non-Christian atmosphere.

''Be assured that I will do anything I can to help you,'' Violet told them, ''but Janie shouldn't have her hopes raised until you know how to proceed." Rising, she said, "If you'll excuse me, I think I have a picture of Janie." She went into the dining room and extracted an album from her desk. She opened it and handed it to the Skeens. "I took that picture of Janie beside her Social Studies exhibit when we were in Springfield a few months ago. It's a good likeness of her."

"She's a pretty girl," Alta said.

"Yes, she is. She was very thin when she enrolled in our school, but she's filled out quite a lot under Mrs. Grady's care. I'm very fond of her."

"Yes, we can tell that, and it goes a long way in making me believe that we could make her happy."

"You've been a big help to us, Miss Conley," Clifford Skeen said as he stood to leave. "I'm pleased Janie has found such a good teacher and friend."

"She's a lovely girl—it's easy to love a girl like Janie."

Three weeks passed, and when Violet didn't have another call from her grandfather, she rested more easily, believing that he had given up on her. Apparently the letter from William O'Brien had convinced Josiah that Violet would not come to live with him. She did feel sorry for the man, that now with the end of his long life in sight, he had no family to share his wealth. He had lived for worldly gain, and in the end it would profit him little. When she thought along this line, she was so relieved that she and Roger had made the choice to live on a modest income, rather than to enjoy "the pleasures of sin for a season," as the biblical writer had stated.

At the school, some of her popularity had dimmed, but when the announcement of her engagement to

Roger was made public, her students looked at her slyly, and especially in the class where Misty was a student, they made cute remarks about her upcoming marriage.

Up until that time, Larry had continued to be friendly, although he had not asked her for another date. When the announcement appeared in the paper, he stopped by the classroom during her preparation period.

"So, you're going through with your marriage to Gibson?" he said.

"Of course. I told you—did you think I was joking?"

"I didn't give it much thought, but I think you can do a lot better. I can offer you a lot more than he ever will."

"That's a matter of opinion—opinions about what traits I value in the man I marry, but that's beside the point. Perhaps I have a short memory," Violet said, "but I can't remember that I've ever had a proposal from you."

Larry's face flushed. "I had planned to ask you to marry me about the time your mother came to live here."

"And you abandoned me at a time when I needed comfort the most! That was when I learned how much I loved Roger—he was my main support during those three months, and I realized he was the kind of man with whom I wanted to share my life."

"But what about your grandfather's wealth? You will need someone to handle your share in his estate. Gibson can't do that."

Staring at him with incredulous eyes, Violet said, "Larry, if you are taking this interest in me because you think I'm going to inherit from my grandfather, let me set the record straight. I have repudiated my grandfather—I want nothing to do with the Conley millions."

"What's going to happen to his fortune? As I understand, you're his only heir."

Violet shrugged her shoulders. "I believe he mentioned donating to charity, but it doesn't matter to me. All I want is for him to continue to ignore me as he has all of my life."

But if Violet wasn't interested in the Conley wealth, she soon learned that others were. Only a week after her frank discussion with Larry, one evening she received a telephone call from Olivia Holland.

"Violet," Mrs. Holland said in her most persuasive tone, "I learned that your grandfather is coming to Saint Louis on a business trip next Thursday, and I invited him to come here to our home for dinner, and afterward to be honored at a reception at the country club, to which I've asked influential people in this section of the state. I want you to be our guest for dinner, and then to stand in the receiving line at the country club."

"Thank you," Violet replied, "but I have another engagement that night." She was going with Roger and his youth group to his farm for a hayride and a wiener roast. "But even if I weren't already committed, I wouldn't accept your invitation—my grandfather and I aren't on good terms and never have been."

Olivia's voice hardened. "I always considered you an intelligent woman."

"I still consider myself intelligent," Violet said calmly, although her heart was pounding like a jack-hammer. "And I prefer not to discuss this subject anymore. Thank you for the invitation, but I must decline.'' She gently replaced the receiver, wondering if anyone else had ever been nervy enough to hang up on Olivia Holland.

And Violet hadn't done it without some trepidation. The Hollands were powerful in this state—powerful enough that they could exert pressure to cause Roger to lose his job, and certainly Larry could make her school employment difficult or nonexistent. She had already considered asking for a transfer, for it was becoming more difficult for her to concentrate on her work when relations were strained between her and Larry.

When she saw Roger, she shared her fears about Olivia interfering in their lives.

''She undoubtedly will,'' he conceded, ''so we should be prepared for it. But with my training, I can go anywhere and find a job, and good teachers are always in demand.''

''Would you mind leaving Maitland?''

''Yes, of course, but I would do that gladly rather than for either of us to kowtow to the Holland factions to keep our jobs. It might be better for us to start our lives over in a new environment anyway. I really don't think it's fair to you to move you into a house I occupied with my first wife. I've wondered if I shouldn't sell that house and buy another.''

''I'm not concerned about it, and Jason and Misty might object.''

''I wouldn't do it without discussing the matter with them, but they might prefer to move, too. I don't want you to ever feel that you're in second place. I loved my wife, but it's over. God has given you to me, and I love you for yourself. It will be a new life for me.''

"Then you're saying it doesn't matter if we do lose our jobs."

"I wouldn't like it because a dismissal would not be good for my record, but I *do* have a good record and several years of seniority. I frankly doubt that the Hollands can touch me, but I'm saying that if we have to choose between our employment and standing up for what we believe is right, we can risk the jobs."

"It's no wonder I love you so much, Roger. A lifetime with you is going to be a pleasure."

So while Olivia Holland entertained Josiah B. Conley and made the headlines of the *Maitland News,* Violet, bundled in a heavy coat and jeans, acted as chaperon to a score of teenagers as the tractor jostled the loaded wagon over the uneven road to a secluded area on the creek bank where a bonfire was built. Until the flames died down, the group sang campfire songs, and then roasted their hotdogs over the glowing coals. More than once, Roger's eyes intercepted Violet's, and he nodded encouragingly. She realized that his mind also was on that other meeting and what repercussions it might have for them. Once he paused by her side, and whispered, "If God is on our side, what can man do to us? Compared to the power of God, the combined forces of Josiah Conley and Olivia Holland are feeble."

Violet was pleased to see that the church youth had dropped many of their reservations about Janie's past, and she was reacting to their friendship as a rose would blossom in the rays of the sun. She strongly suspected that one of the boys had developed a romantic interest in Janie.

When Violet wandered away from the campfire, so

she could look up at the numerous stars in the darkness, Janie followed her.

"Miss Conley, I've had some news that could be bad, but I'm hoping for the best. Mrs. Grady has learned from the social agency that someone is asking questions about me and I'm hoping it's my father."

"That would be wonderful, Janie," was the only answer Violet could give because she didn't want to raise the girl's hopes and then have her disappointed if her father couldn't take her. She wished they had some way to know what had happened to Janie's mother. "I'm praying for you, dear."

Violet spent the rest of the evening contemplating Janie's future to forestall any thoughts of her own paternal heritage, for she couldn't dispel the feeling that Josiah Conley wasn't finished with her yet.

Since they were considering the purchase of a new house, Roger and Violet decided to put Violet's house up for sale and use the proceeds from it as a down payment on a new house when they selected one. On Saturday morning, they were showing the house to a real estate agent, when Violet looked out the window to see a sleek limousine pulling gingerly into her driveway.

Her muttered, "Oh, no," brought Roger to her side immediately.

"Josiah Conley?" he said. Violet nodded.

"Are you going to talk with him?"

"I might as well—he won't leave me alone until I do, and maybe not then."

"The real estate agent is about finished anyway, so I'll ask him to do some figuring and telephone you on

Monday with his proposed sale price. Do you want me to leave, too?"

"No, I won't talk with him alone. He intimidates me."

When the doorbell rang, Violet murmured a short prayer for guidance before she opened the door. Her grandfather was accompanied by his secretary, Miss Whitaker. Violet unlocked the storm door and motioned for them to enter.

"Please be seated," she said. "May I offer you a cup of coffee?"

"No, we've breakfasted," Josiah declined; but the secretary looked as if she might have welcomed something.

Josiah took Violet's chair, and she sat on the couch beside Miss Whitaker.

"Why have you been avoiding me? Why haven't you answered my calls?" Josiah said, putting Violet on the defensive immediately.

"After I notified you that I wasn't interested in the position you were offering me, I didn't consider that we had anything to discuss."

"Did you really think that I would take your answer as final? I'm willing to negotiate with you—what more do you want?"

The kitchen door closed behind the real estate agent, and Violet sensed Roger's presence in the room. She turned in his direction.

Standing, she said, "Roger, let me introduce you to Josiah B. Conley. This is my fiancé, Roger Gibson." She moved to Roger's side, and he put an arm around her waist.

Josiah looked Roger up and down, and Roger stood patiently under the sharp scrutiny. Since he was going to work in an hour, he was wearing his uniform, and he presented an awesome bearing. "Well, you've picked a man," Josiah conceded at last. "I was given to understand that you were interested in Larry Holland."

Roger continued to stand, but Violet resumed her seat on the couch.

"Not any more. When my mother came here to live, he dropped me like a hot potato, and didn't show any more interest until he learned I was related to you. He doesn't want me—he's interested in your wealth."

"Which shows that he's a wise man," Josiah said, making Violet realize that this characteristic of Larry's elevated him in her grandfather's estimation.

Josiah turned to Roger. "Are you the one who persuaded Violet to turn down a handsome position as my granddaughter and sole heir?"

"No, sir—Violet made that decision alone, but I support her stand."

"I've had both of you investigated," Josiah said, "and as my heirs, you would make more money in a month than you do now in a year. Doesn't that interest you?"

"No, sir," Roger said. "I have all I need now."

"What if I told you that I have a nephew who is more than willing to step in and take what you're rejecting?" Josiah said to Violet, his eyes piercing in their intensity.

She smiled. "That would make me very happy, for I am sorry that I had to reject your offer—not sorry for myself, but for you because I thought you had no one else to turn to. Your nephew seems like a good solution to your problem."

"Well, you've had your chance," Josiah said, rising

from the chair. "I don't have to beg anyone to be my heir. Anyway, I doubt I would be happy having a murderess's daughter bear my grandchildren."

Violet started angrily, and Roger moved swiftly to her side, his arm on her shoulder suggesting caution. She swallowed twice before she had the strength to ignore the insult.

"That is my opinion, too," Violet said quietly. "And since you've brought up my mother, I want to tell you that there will be a documentary about her crime, trial, imprisonment and death on "Travesty of Justice" in two weeks. You may want to watch it."

Anger changed his features. "How dare you! I will not have the Conley name sullied. I'll block that broadcast."

"I doubt you can do that," Violet said. "All of the information they use is available to the public, except for some court documents, which I have authorized them to use."

"How dare you!" Josiah repeated, and started toward Violet, his hands clenched at his side. Roger stepped in front of her.

"It's time for you to leave, Mr. Conley," he said quietly and firmly, but his eyes glittered dangerously. "Violet has made her position plain. She doesn't want to have any further contact with you."

"I'll sue to stop that program, or anything else I have to do."

Feeling that Josiah had conquered his desire to harm her, Violet stood beside Roger again. "My lawyer is William O'Brien, in Kansas City. You can reach me through him if you have any further need to contact me," Violet said. "You've spent almost a quarter of a century without recognizing me, and I really don't feel that it would have worked out. I now have the full facts of what caused Mother to kill her husband and how you railroaded her into prison, and I can never forget that, although my Christian beliefs have led me to forgive you. When I was a child, I would have welcomed some attention from you, but it's too late now. I believe we will both be happier if we continue as we have in the past.''

''You'll be sorry,'' Josiah said, as he headed for the door, curtly motioning for his secretary to follow him. Miss Whitaker gave Violet a compassionate glance before she left the house. Violet turned into Roger's arms and put her head on his shoulder.

''Will he leave us alone now?''

''I think so,'' Roger answered slowly. ''I read defeat in his eyes when you said you would have liked some attention when you were a child.''

''I only hope I can put all of this behind me. I don't want anything to interfere with our chances for a happy marriage.''

''I'm not worried about that, nor should you be. Don't forget our Lord's words when he cautioned, 'Therefore do not worry about tomorrow, for tomorrow will worry about itself.' I've given a lot of prayerful thought to our marriage, searching the Bible for assurance that we've made the right decision, and over and over I keep returning to the incident in the Old Testament when Joshua challenged the Israelites to serve God, and more than once, I've made the same pledge Joshua did, 'But as for me and my household, we will serve the Lord.'''

''You're right, of course, and I do trust most of the time, but I have my moments of weakness, and the overwhelming personality of Josiah Conley causes my courage to dwindle. When I worry about what he and the Hollands might do to us, I keep reminding myself of the Apostle Paul's words to the Romans, 'For I am convinced that neither death nor life, neither angels nor demons, neither the present nor the future, nor any powers, neither height nor depth, nor anything else in all creation, will be able to separate us from the love of God that is in Christ Jesus our Lord.''"

"That's the way to believe," Roger assured her. "I'm not anticipating a carefree future, and we can expect to face difficulties, but we need to hold on to the truth that with God on our side, nothing will come our way that we can't handle together."

"That word *together* is a powerful antidote for trouble," Violet agreed. "Only a short time until that's a reality."

Chapter Eleven

Roger and Violet had agreed upon a simple wedding with only Misty and Jason as their attendants, and on Thursday night, Violet invited the three Gibsons for supper, and afterward, they would make plans for the ceremony. She prepared a large pan of lasagna, a garden salad, garlic bread, and tried her hand at a blueberry pie, which she would serve warm with frozen vanilla yogurt. Her hands trembled as she extended the dining room table and laid four place settings, realizing that this would be the normal eating arrangement when she acquired her new family. She had seldom prepared a meal for more than two people, although she had learned to cook under Aunt Ruth's tutelage. What if the children didn't like her cooking?

By the time the Gibsons arrived, she was edgy, to the extent that she caught herself nibbling on her fingernails. She took a deep breath when she heard the pickup pull into the driveway. Misty and Jason breezed into the house in an argument over the merits of their favorite soccer teams.

"Smells good in here," Jason commented. "Pie!" he said, when he spied the pastry cooling on the cabinet.

"Put your jackets in the closet," Violet instructed. "The food will be ready in ten minutes."

"Okay if we turn on the television?" Misty asked. "Sure."

Roger entered the kitchen, and she turned frightened eyes toward him. He put his arms around her and bent for a kiss, and she darted anxious eyes toward the living room. He had never caressed her in front of his children.

As his lips hovered over hers, he murmured, "They might as well get used to seeing me kiss you. I intend to do it quite often."

She was rigid in his arms, and he said, "Is something wrong?"

"What if they don't like the way I cook?"

He laughed at her. "They've eaten my cooking for years, and I haven't heard many complaints. You're going to make a great mother—stop fretting about it."

Violet looked toward the living room where Jason's developing frame filled her lounge chair. "I hope so, but it's intimidating to become a mother to someone who's only six years younger than I am."

"He's still a kid at heart, believe me. Want me to help you?"

"The salads are in the fridge. You can put them on the table, and put ice in the glasses. I have pitchers of fruit punch or tea—you can have a choice."

But Violet stopped worrying about her culinary abilities when Jason scraped the last of the lasagna out of the baking dish and said, "Dad, you surely do know how to pick 'em. Not only did you choose a beauty, but she's a great cook, too!''

''Well, if you want me to give you some pointers on finding a girlfriend, you only have to ask. You haven't been doing so well on your own,'' Roger countered.

Jason groaned.

''It was a good meal,'' Misty said when they had finished their pie. ''Dad is a good meat and potatoes cook, but he won't try his hand in the bakery department.'' She stood up. ''Now, it's my turn to work. The rest of you guys go into the living room—I know how to load a dishwasher.''

''All right,'' Violet said, at Roger's nod. ''The dishwashing liquid is under the sink. Let me know if you need any help.''

By the time Misty finished, the evening news was over, and Violet turned off the television. She brought a notepad from her desk and curled up on the couch beside Roger since Jason was comfortable in her usual chair. Misty took a cushion from the couch and sat on the floor near them.

''Roger and I thought that the two of you should be involved in planning the wedding service,'' she said. ''Where do we start?''

The telephone rang, and Violet laughed. ''That figures! I seldom sit down that the phone doesn't ring.''

As she started toward the desk to answer, Roger said, ''If you think your phone rings a lot, wait until you live in a house with two teenagers. I gave up fighting with them for phone time and installed two phones. They aren't allowed to receive calls on my phone.''

''We like it that way, Dad,'' Misty assured him.

When Violet lifted the receiver, Mrs. Grady's worried tones filled her ear.

"I'm sorry to bother you, Miss Conley, but Janie hasn't come home yet. At first, I supposed she might be helping one of the teachers, although she usually tells me. But now that it's so late, I'm worried. Is she at your house?"

A wave of apprehension swept over Violet. "Why, no—I haven't seen her since she left my class in early afternoon, although sometimes she does stop in at the close of the day. Just a minute. Misty Gibson is here now, I'll ask her if she knows anything." Violet lowered the phone. "Mrs. Grady says that Janie hasn't come home yet. Do you have any idea where she might be, Misty?"

Misty shook her head. "She was in last period class, and we left the school building at the same time. She started down the street as she always does—I assumed that she was going home."

Roger came to Violet's side as she relayed the message to Mrs. Grady. Violet held the phone so he could hear Mrs. Grady's answer.

"I was gone at the time Janie usually comes home, for I had to pick up the little ones at their school. She apparently entered the house, for her book bag is lying on the table in the hallway."

Roger took the phone. "Mrs. Grady, this is Roger Gibson. I'll be right over to talk with you. In the meantime, check to see if any of her clothing is gone."

When he replaced the receiver, Violet said, "I'm going with you." He nodded his head.

"Jason, you and Misty can go home in the pickup. We can use Violet's car."

Misty eyes were worried. "Do you suppose she's run away again?" she whispered.

"I can't believe it," Violet said, "but that's what most people will think." Violet felt devastated. And confused. Since Clifford Skeen had started arrangements to assume custody of Janie the girl had been delighted. It just didn't make sense that she'd run away again.

Mrs. Grady, a robust, florid-complexioned woman, met them at the door, her eyes tearful, her face strained with concern.

"As far as I can determine, nothing is gone except the clothes she wore this morning. I know she came into the house because of the book bag, but there's no other sign that she's been here. Usually, she has a glass of milk as soon as she comes home, but there's no empty glass in the sink. I'm really concerned."

"Calm yourself, Mrs. Grady," Roger said, taking her arm and leading her to a chair in the living room, where the two small children were watching television. Without permission, he turned down the volume. "Have you contacted any of her friends?"

"I telephoned a few of the people she's met at your teen group before I bothered Miss Conley, but none of them has seen her. As you know, she hasn't made many friends." Mrs. Grady pulled a tissue from her apron pocket and wiped her eyes. "I can't believe that the child would run away—she has seemed happy, looking forward so much to living with her father."

Violet took Mrs. Grady's hand. "She has been contented, and excited over the prospects that she might find her father. I don't believe that she would run away—she hated living on the streets. But I shudder at the alternative. If she didn't leave voluntarily, has she been kidnapped?''

"That thought terrifies me," Mrs. Grady admitted. "I'm always gone for a half hour at the same time each afternoon to bring the children from school. If someone was watching Janie, they would know that she was alone here."

"But there's no sign of a struggle," Roger said. "She wouldn't have gone voluntarily if she didn't know the person."

"Yes, but it could have been someone we know," Mrs. Grady said. "Janie can be so trusting."

"Perhaps it will relieve your mind to know that there's very little chance any serious crime has occurred here in Maitland," he said. He rose from the couch. "You stay here by the phone, and I'll go to headquarters and see what I can learn. If we don't hear anything in a few hours, we'll put out an APB on her. We should also contact Clifford Skeen. Perhaps Janie decided to go to him."

"Do you want me to stay with you tonight?" Violet asked.

"No, I'll be all right. She may try to telephone you if she's in trouble," Mrs. Grady said. "You should be near your telephone."

Violet drove Roger to the police headquarters, and when he got out of the car, he said, "Don't worry too much. There may be a perfectly logical explanation."

"But I'm devastated—just when it seemed that life was straightening out for Janie, this has to happen."

Roger squeezed her hand. "I'll do everything possible."

The night seemed long to Violet, and she couldn't imagine how long it must have been for Janie, wherever the poor child was. Since Roger hadn't telephoned, she knew he hadn't learned anything, and on her way to school, she stopped by Mrs. Grady's home.

"I've haven't had any news at all," Violet said when Janie's foster mother quickly opened the door. She obviously hadn't slept, and her eyes were red from fatigue and crying.

"I heard something," Mrs. Grady said. "My neighbor across the street is an invalid, and she spends a lot of time in her wheelchair by the window. She says she has noticed a strange car driving slowly along the street this week. She always naps in the afternoon, so she wasn't at the window when Janie came home from school. Do you think that could be important?"

"At this point, we shouldn't overlook any possibility. Contact Lieutenant Gibson today and give him the information. Did your neighbor note anything about the car?"

"Only that it was a red compact of some kind, rather old. But she didn't see the driver."

"That isn't much to go on, but we don't have anything else."

When Violet drove into the school's parking lot, Roger was dropping Misty off for classes. He strode toward Violet, and in spite of her worry about Janie, her heart somersaulted at the sight of him. What a man!

"I stayed at headquarters until midnight," he said, "but we didn't have any information then, and I left instructions to telephone about any new developments. I'm on my way to work now. Ask kids at school about Janie, her mood lately, anything she might have said about living with her father. Try to learn anything you can."

Violet did her best to check with anyone Janie had talked with the day before, but she didn't uncover any information that would have caused the girl to run away. Ironically, in Janie's absence, she received more attention than she did when she was present, and her name was on everyone's tongue before the day ended.

Violet's feet were dragging when she reached home at the end of the day. The light was flashing on her answering machine, and wanting nothing more than to stretch out on the bed, she considered ignoring the message until she had rested. Curiosity overrode her fatigue, and Violet slouched on a chair and punched the button.

"One message," the automated machine sounded. "I-57 North. My mother—" The message stopped abruptly. Violet sat upright, fatigue forgotten. She replayed the message. Although the words were muffled, there was no doubt it was Janie's voice. Excitedly, Violet dialed the police headquarters and was heady with relief when Roger answered.

She repeated the message, and he said, "What time was the message received?"

"Twenty minutes after noon."

"That's the interstate between Mount Vernon and Chicago, so no doubt they're in Chicago by now, but we'll find them. I was beginning to wonder if Janie's mother wasn't involved. I couldn't imagine anyone else that she would go with willingly."

"Why would she wait so long to come for Janie if she wanted her?"

"She probably didn't know where Janie was until the social agency started making inquiries on Clifford's behalf—who incidentally didn't know anything and is quite concerned. I'll feed this new information into the system, and we should know something soon.''

Violet placed a call to Mrs. Grady before she collapsed on her bed. Although still concerned about Janie's welfare, it could have been worse. At least, she didn't believe Janie's mother would intentionally harm her, but association with the woman would disrupt Janie's life again.

Violet was still asleep on Friday morning when Roger telephoned at six-thirty.

''We've found her,'' he said. ''Janie's mother has a record, and the Chicago police knew where she lived. They watched the area until Pat Skeen and a male companion showed up with Janie, who was taken and placed in the custody of a social agency in Chicago. I'm going after her tomorrow. Do you want to go along?''

''Of course I'll come. Janie is probably very upset, and she'll need a friend.'' Violet felt so relieved that Janie had been found, but her heart went out to the poor girl who now had to deal with so many conflicting emotions.

''This is an official duty, so we'll go in a police cruiser. I'll pick you up at seven o'clock.''

Violet hadn't considered that she could have any greater regard for Roger, but on the trip to Chicago, her admiration increased. When they arrived in Chicago, he exuded an air of efficiency and confidence that commanded respect when he entered the headquarters of the troopers who had located Janie.

In a short time, they had received the necessary papers to return Janie to Maitland, and two local state policemen accompanied them to the social facility where the girl had been housed overnight. Apparently Janie hadn't been told that they were coming after her, for when they entered the room where she was slumped in a chair, looking out the window, she stared in amazement for a minute before she ran toward Violet's open arms.

"Miss Conley! How did you find me?"

"Your call to me was the clue we needed. We've come to take you back to Maitland, Janie. What happened? Why did you leave with your mother without a word to any of us?"

"She came to the door right after I got home Thursday. I invited her in, but she said that she couldn't stay, and had only recently learned where I was and that she had brought my clothes and other things. I didn't have many clothes, but I did have a collection of stuffed dogs that I had missed, so I went down to the car with her to get them. There was a man in the car, and he pulled me inside, and they drove away with me."

"We've all been frantic about you, but that telephone call put us on the right track."

"We stopped at a restaurant, and when I went to the restroom, I found a phone. I put in that call for you, but my mother's companion caught me and hung up before I could tell you much."

"That was enough," Roger said. "We have the papers for your release, and we want to return to Maitland today. Are you ready to go?"

"I guess so—I have nothing to take, but could I see my mother before we leave? She looks terrible," Janie added in a worried voice.

"We can't take you there unless we receive permission from the agency," Roger replied.

When he checked with the woman on duty in the office, she told him, "We've been trying to get Janie's mother to sign papers giving Clifford Skeen full custody, but she's refused. Perhaps you could persuade her, but I don't want you to go there alone. I'll contact one of our male workers who knows where Mrs. Skeen lives, and he will go along, thus making the visit official. And, of course, you must take the two police officers—it isn't a desirable neighborhood."

"We'll take Janie across the street for lunch while we wait," Roger said.

Janie didn't have much appetite and merely nibbled at the hamburger before her. "I feel sorry for my mother," she admitted, "but I can't live with her. She doesn't know what she's doing most of the time. If you hadn't found me, I would have run away again as soon as she passed out to try to find my way back to Maitland."

"Then why do you want to see her?" Violet asked.

"I don't know—maybe to convince her that I don't want to live with her. Maybe just to say goodbye," she added quietly.

Violet's heart ached to witness Janie's distress, but she couldn't close her mind to the dreadful environment when they entered the neighborhood where Janie's mother lived. How had the sweet-natured, gentle Janie ever been nurtured under conditions like these?

The man from the social agency followed in his car, but when the cruiser crawled to a stop in front of an eight-story building, the streets emptied of people although Violet sensed that watchful eyes peered from every window and dark corner. The two local policemen stayed with the cruiser, and Violet appreciated

Roger's vigilance as the social agent came to their side and said, "Mrs. Skeen lives on the third floor. We'll have to walk. There's no elevator."

"Is this where you lived when you ran away?" Violet asked.

"No, we were living in Springfield at the time. I don't know when she came here."

"Were your surroundings always as bad as this?"

Janie smiled slightly. "Sometimes worse, although we did have a nice apartment occasionally. But we were always on the move."

A woman in a dirty, ragged terry cloth robe opened the door to their knock. In a faded, worn manner, the woman resembled Janie, so Violet knew this was Pat Skeen.

"Decided to bring my daughter back to me, have you? You had no right to take her in the first place."

"We've been through this before," the agent said. "You abandoned your daughter, and when we found her wandering on the streets of this city more dead than alive, we had not only the right, but an obligation, to rescue her from the dangers she faced."

Pat said nothing. She looked down, then glanced up at Janie. For an instant Violet thought she saw a flash of tenderness in the woman's cold stare. "Your daughter is being taken back to Maitland and her foster home there, but she wanted to see you before she left."

Pat stepped aside, and they entered a sparsely furnished one-room apartment with a small kitchenette and bath.

"We can't stay long, Janie," Roger said. "We have a long drive ahead of us, so tell your mother what you want to, so we can be on our way."

"Who are these people, Janie?" Pat asked.

Janie took Violet's hand. "This is my teacher, Miss Conley, who has been very good to me. Lieutenant Gibson is a state policeman in our town. He was sent to return me to Maitland."

She didn't release Violet's hand, and Violet returned the girl's tight grip. "Mother, please don't try to take me away again. My foster mother is very good to me, and now that I've seen how normal people live, I can't come back to a place like this."

"Can't say that I blame you, but it's the best I have to offer. I wouldn't have come after you this time, but I thought you might have been taken against your will."

"No. I was so miserable when the social workers found me, that I was happy to find someone to take me in."

"What's this about your father wanting you?"

"I told you yesterday. He learned from your sister that I was his daughter and he wants me to live with him."

"What kind of wife does he have?"

"I haven't seen her—Miss Conley has."

"She impressed me as a kind, good-hearted woman, and she does want to take Janie," Violet said. "She isn't doing this for Clifford. She *wants* to give Janie a good home."

"And it's your opinion that they'll be good for Janie?"

Violet nodded. "She desperately needs the security of a decent home."

Pat looked at the social worker. "If you have those papers here, I'll sign them."

"Mrs. Skeen," Violet said. "Forgive me for giving

unsolicited advice, but why don't you come with us? Clifford told me that your family is concerned about you. I'm sure they will give you help to recover from your problems. I think Clifford would do it himself, for Janie's sake. Why don't you make an effort to change your life?''

Pat smiled wryly as she took the paper the social worker gave her and leaned over to sign it. ''It's too late. That's the only reason I'm agreeing to let Janie go. You might not believe it, but I love my daughter. Forget this life, Janie, and go with your father. Clifford was always a decent sort—that's the reason we didn't get along.''

Janie started to embrace her mother, but Pat backed away and shook her head. Janie turned to Violet, who put her arm around the girl's shoulder and comforted her as she began to cry.

It was a somber group that walked down the hallway to the stairs. Violet turned for one last look, and knew she would never forget the forlorn figure of Pat Skeen, leaning against the door jamb watching their departure with a hand to her throbbing throat.

Chapter Twelve

Peter Pierce scheduled Linda's story for the second Saturday night in May. Since it was the night before Mother's Day, Violet considered it an appropriate time for the telecast. Feeling that it might be a traumatic time for her, she invited Pastor Tom to come to her home and watch the program with her and Roger.

But the situation was handled with diplomacy and tact. Ryan Conley was portrayed as a man with a troubled mind, rather than a sadistic husband. Linda was depicted as a woman driven to murder when her husband had threatened their child. It was difficult to hear the tragic story of her parents' marriage, but as they watched Roger sat with his strong arm around her shoulders, and with his other hand, he caressed her tense fingers.

When the program ended, Violet clicked the remote control. The three of them sat in silence for several minutes.

"Violet, you should be commended for allowing the revelation of this tragedy that took your parents away from you," Pastor Tom said. "It couldn't have been an easy decision to allow your parents' problems to be broadcast to the world, but it certainly vindicated Linda's action, while at the same time leniently portraying your father as a man with psychological problems rather than as a mean-spirited person."

"Yes, he must have been mentally unbalanced," Roger said. "No sane man would behave in such a manner."

"Of course, Mr. O'Brien is prejudiced against my grandfather, but he said that my parents were happy the first years of their marriage, and that the trouble started when they moved back to Kansas City and my grandfather tightened his hold on my father."

"Quite likely," Pastor Tom agreed. He smiled. "I hope you can put the past behind you now."

"I intend to. We're getting married soon, and I want to concentrate on that now."

"You are two people who should need little marriage counseling, but I'll want a session with you as with all others I marry, so be sure to schedule a few hours for that."

After the pastor left, Roger said, "I've talked with Jason and Misty, and both of them are agreeable to selling our home to move into a different house. My house is paid for, and you have some equity built up in yours, so we should have a good sum to buy another house when we pool our resources."

Violet nodded. "Can we afford one of the new houses in that subdivision north of town? They seem spacious, but we'll need a large house because we're starting out with a family of four."

"Let's look at them tomorrow afternoon. I noticed in the newspaper that an open house is scheduled, and a few of the houses are ready for immediate occupancy."

"Good idea. We should take Jason and Misty along. We don't want them to feel left out."

The next day, the four of them ate at a buffet restaurant at noon, and were on hand when the houses at Colonial Acres opened to the public at two o'clock. The colonial-style houses were being built on one-acre lots, and three were completed and ready for viewing. It was the last house they checked out that pleased all of them.

The dwelling was a modified two-story Dutch colonial with cream-colored siding and brown shingled roof. The first floor had a large family room, kitchen, dining area and a living room that ran the width of the house. A utility room and lavatory occupied an area near the garage entry. Three bedrooms and two baths were on the second floor, and a studio loft and a smaller room, designated as a sewing area, were located over the garage.

Jason immediately preempted the studio for his bedroom.

"But there's no bathroom up here, Jason," Misty said.

"No trouble for Dad and me to install a small bathroom when I return from Europe. The few days I'm here before then, I can use that small one downstairs. Okay, Dad?"

Roger looked at Violet, and she nodded. "That should work out great, leaving one bedroom for guests when your family comes to visit, Roger, or when Aunt Ruth is here."

"Or, for a nursery when the time comes," Roger

added with a smile. Violet had thought the same, but didn't want to say it aloud.

The master bedroom with its large bath and walk-in closet was spacious enough for Roger and Violet, and Misty liked the larger of the other two rooms. After their inspection of the house, the four of them sat on the carpeted floor of the living room to discuss their options.

"I suppose we should consider the most important question, Dad," Jason said. "Can we afford a house like this?" His statement pleased Violet—mature thinking for a nineteen-year-old. Roger had done his work well.

"Not if I had to pay for it alone," he said, "but with Violet working, we should be able to swing it. It depends somewhat on how much we can get for our two houses. If the cost is so great that I can't afford to send you to college, then we'll stay where we are."

"I fully intend to work and pay for most of my own college expenses," Jason said, "that way you'll only have Misty to support. After I take this trip through Europe, I want to work for a year if you approve. It may take several years to graduate, but if I finance my own education, I'll appreciate it more."

"Of course, you have the trust fund we set up with your mother's insurance that will be an income for both of you when you're each twenty-one. That will help quite a lot." Roger turned to Violet. "What's your opinion?"

"I like the house, and we shouldn't have to buy any furniture when we combine what we have in both houses. My vote is to purchase."

"I'm agreeable, too," Roger said. "Misty, we've heard from everyone except you."

"Can we be moved in before the wedding?" she asked.

"That depends on the contractor and how fast our houses sell. Six weeks should give us time."

"I would like to move my bedroom before the wedding, and since Jason is leaving the next day for Europe, he should move his things, too." She dropped her head. "You see, Dad, I want to go back with Grandma to spend the summer in Arizona, if you will let me. Now don't get me wrong, for I want you to marry Miss Conley, but I would rather be gone the first few weeks when you're…getting used to one another."

Her face flushed, and Roger and Violet exchanged an understanding smile.

"I've already asked Grandma, and she said it would be fine if you'll permit it. She agrees that it would be better for the two of you to be alone this summer."

"That's thoughtful of you, Misty," Violet said, "although I hadn't thought of such a thing. I don't want either of you to ever feel that I don't want you in the house."

"We don't feel that way," Jason assured her. "As soon as the two of you say, 'I do,' I'm going to start calling you Mother," Jason said. "I'll think of you like that while I'm gone, and it will be natural for me when we're together as a family again. Our first mother was 'Mama' to us."

Roger clasped his arm around Jason in an affectionate gesture. "By all means, Misty, go with your grandmother for the summer. It's considerate of you to give Violet and me some space. It was her idea to bring the two of you along to view this house and help make a decision, so she wants you around, and I wouldn't

marry anyone who wasn't willing to share my kids—
you know that. I love Violet very much, but that
doesn't lessen my love for you, nor will it change our
feelings for you if we have more children, as we expect to."

Before they left the house, the four of them huddled
together in a mutual embrace as Roger prayed. "Lord,
we remember the words from the Bible,
'Every...house divided against itself shall not stand,
and Unless the Lord builds the house, its builders labor
in vain.' I can't find the words to tell you how grateful
I am that you've given me two such understanding
children and Violet, who not only is possessed of a
heart big enough for me, but is willing to accept Misty
and Jason as well. The day when their mother died,
the three of us thought we could never find happiness
again, but in your wisdom, you've brought Violet into
our lives. Thank you, God. We praise you with our
lips and our lives. Amen."

All four of them cried, hugged and kissed in a moment that would prove as sacred as the marriage ceremony. Their wedding day would serve to confirm the
pledges they made here today, for it was fitting that in
this building that would become their home, they had
become a family.

The next month passed in a flurry of activities that
kept Violet and Roger so busy that they had little time
to be alone. The Realtor from whom they bought the
new house worked out a package deal—if he couldn't
sell their two houses by the time they wanted to move,
he would take them as a payment on their new home.
While Violet was busy the first two weeks of June
with school-closing activities, Roger and his children

moved into the new house and started living there. Violet wouldn't move her furniture until after they were married. When Aunt Ruth arrived for the wedding, she would stay with Violet in her old home.

After many hours of soul-searching, Violet asked Larry for an appointment during her prep period. The two of them sat in painful silence for several minutes.

Taking a deep breath, Violet said, "I've decided to apply for a transfer to Maitland Middle School when the school year starts in September."

Larry nervously snapped the top of the ballpoint pen he held and kept his eyes on the desk pad before him.

"You're a good teacher, Violet—I'll hate to lose you."

"Then if my work has been satisfactory, I hope that you will give me a good recommendation and not hinder the transfer."

He looked at her in amazement. "What makes you think I would do anything as petty as that? Have I ever treated you unfairly?"

Perhaps the Hollands were above revenge and not vindictive as she and Roger had feared. "Not professionally, no, and I apologize for that inference. I have always liked teaching here, but the situation has been a bit strained during this semester, and for the good of both of us, I believe I should leave. Also, it might be intimidating for Misty to have a stepmother on the staff."

"You can be assured that I will do anything in my power to grant your wishes," Larry said genially.

Violet stood to conclude the interview. "Larry, I don't know if I should say this, but I remember fondly the times we had together. We were good friends, but

I'm sure that both of us are better off that the relationship didn't go any further.''

''You may be right, although right now, I can't see that. I'm fond of you, Violet, but apparently it wasn't meant to be. I hope that you will be happy.''

Violet wiped unshed tears from her eyes as she left the room.

Violet and Misty, who was going to be maid of honor, went to Saint Louis one Saturday to shop for wedding clothes. Since she couldn't have her mother with her for the wedding, Violet decided to use some of the money she had inherited from Linda to buy her dress, for she wanted to feel that her mother had a part in the wedding. They went to an exclusive shop, and she chose a venise lace empire cage dress with allover embroidered illusion sleeves and chapel train topping a satin gown. The matching shoulder-length veil was attached to a small crown of pearls. Violet knew she didn't have any jewelry worthy of such a gown, but after the expense of the dress, veil, and white satin shoes, she wasn't going to buy jewelry. Actually, the dress didn't need any ornamentation, and her pearl earrings would suffice.

For Misty they chose a pink sleeveless rosette-back organza A-line with a matching organza wrap, which set off her blond features.

The open church informal wedding was to be held at six o'clock with a reception following in the church's fellowship room for all the guests. At her insistence, Aunt Ruth would assume the cost of the reception, and they planned for two hundred guests.

Roger was spending all of his free time in moving,

but after Violet's school year ended, he dropped in occasionally on his noon hour, and they lunched together.

One day, he said, "I've neglected to talk with you about a honeymoon. Is there any place in particular you would like to go?"

"I didn't suppose we could afford to go away, so I hadn't given it any thought."

"I'd like for us to be alone for a while."

"Of course we'll be alone all summer after the children leave." Violet thought for a few minutes. "Why don't we go out to your farm for a couple of days? We could have all the privacy we want there."

"Say," Roger said, and his eyes lighted into a smile, "I would like that."

Aunt Ruth arrived the day before the wedding. Not concerned about it being "bad luck" to see the groom on the day of the wedding, Violet invited Roger to have breakfast with her and Ruth.

They had just finished their scrambled eggs, bacon, toast and juice when the doorbell rang. Still holding a teacup in her hand, Violet went to the front door and opened it to—Josiah B. Conley. His limousine was parked in front of the house.

They stared at one another for a few seconds before Violet unlatched the screen door and motioned her grandfather to enter. He carried a large case.

"Would you like some breakfast?" she said. She indicated the dining area. "We had just finished."

"No, thank you. I've eaten."

Motioning for Ruth and Roger to join them, she asked her grandfather to be seated.

"You've met Roger," she said, "But this is my

aunt, Ruth Reed—she's the one who gave me a home and reared me."

Josiah gave Ruth an appraising glance. "Then I must commend her for doing the task well."

Ruth acknowledged the compliment with a nod. It was obvious that she was uncomfortable in his company.

Violet took Roger's hand so that he would sit beside her on the couch. She was amazed at how much calmer she felt in her grandfather's presence than she had when he had been here before. He couldn't intimidate her anymore. This time tomorrow she would be Mrs. Roger Gibson, and she considered that a highly potent buffer against intimidation.

"Well, Violet," Josiah said. "I've taken you at your word. I've made my brother's son my heir. He's worked at Midwest Enterprises for several years, so he already knows much about the business, and by the time I die, he should be well qualified to handle my estate as I want it done. He already has three sons, so the family operation should be ensured for many years to come."

Violet smiled warmly. "I'm very pleased about that. I didn't enjoy refusing you, but the Conley dynasty held no fascination for me. I'm used to a simpler life. I would have been unhappy."

Josiah sighed. "As I've told you before, you remind me of my Rachel, and I would have liked you in my home. But," he added with a wry smile, "she was meek most of the time, though occasionally she refused me, too, and did what she wanted to do." A softer light came into his eyes as he reflected on the wife he had loved, and he took an envelope from the inside pocket of his coat. "I didn't know I had a conscience," he said, "but I apparently do, because I will no longer withhold from you this letter discovered in Rachel's possessions after her death."

He handed Rachel the business-size envelope labeled, "To my granddaughter, Violet." As she stared at the envelope with wondering eyes, Josiah lifted a large jewelry chest from the case he carried—it was the one Violet had seen at his home in Kansas City. "You were also mentioned in her will. Rachel wanted you to have her jewelry."

Josiah opened the chest, and placed it on the coffee table. Sunlight coming through the window sparkled brightly on a vast display of diamonds, rubies, gold and silver jewelry. Violet picked up the ornate necklace that she had worn to the reception in the Conley mansion. Noting that Violet was speechless, Josiah said, "Perhaps you will have a daughter to inherit these some day. Many of these items have been in Rachel's family since the War Between the States."

"My life-style doesn't call for jewelry of this magnitude, but I can assure you that I will cherish the gift and keep it for the next generation." She took a letter opener from the table and slit the seal on the envelope, holding the letter so that Roger could see the message as she read silently.

My dearest granddaughter,

You *are* dear to me, although I am not allowed to have any communication with you. You are all that is left to me of my favorite son, and although I do not hold him blameless for his actions, he was mine and I loved him. Your mother was a wonderful woman. We were close, and I have mourned her and miss her as I would have a daughter.

Although Josiah forbade me to have any contact with you, I have never forgotten your birthday, and on each of those days and on Christmas, I have added gift money to a trust fund I started for you on your third birthday. This is money that I inherited from my mother, and over which my husband had no control.

I am dying, and I only pray that Josiah will pass this letter on to you; otherwise, you will never know that my love for you never wavered. I pray that God will bless you.

Your grandmother, Rachel Conley

At the bottom of the letter was the name of a bank in Saint Louis and an account number. The trust fund was in the name of Violet Conley, with Rachel Conley as trustee until her death.

"Do you know what the letter says?" Violet asked her grandfather.

"I haven't stooped to reading other people's letters," he said tersely.

Violet handed him the letter, and although his face remained impassive as he read, when he finished, he had to clear his throat several times before he spoke.

"I suspected something of the sort because when we settled her estate, a great deal of money was gone, but it was her money and she had the right to do what she wanted with it."

Roger and Ruth sat without speaking, but Roger laid his hand on Violet's shoulder.

"Do you know the size of this trust fund?" she asked.

"I have no idea," Josiah said, "but it won't be

difficult for you to find out by calling the bank and giving that account number. I would judge there could be upward of a quarter of a million dollars.''

Violet gasped. ''It seems I'm bound to have money thrust upon me whether I want it or not.'' She looked at Roger. ''What should I do?''

''Whatever you want, but if you're thinking this bequest will make any difference in our relationship, it won't. Since this is a trust fund, I imagine you'll find out that it's one that passes from one generation to another, and you will receive the interest rather than the capital itself. Admittedly, even that will make our lives a lot easier, but not a large enough amount to intimidate me.'' He looked at Josiah, who nodded.

''I'm sure that is the case—Rachel had a good head on her shoulders, and she had no idea how Violet would turn out. It's doubtful that she would have handed the money to her carte blanche.''

''It seems I'm destined to have a rich wife, no matter how hard I've fought it,'' Roger said, and he playfully ruffled Violet's short hair. ''You've turned down two fortunes to marry me, but I remember the old cliché, 'The third time is the charm.' I believe you're justified in accepting this one.''

Josiah lifted his shaggy eyebrows. ''*Two* fortunes?''

''Besides what she would have gained as your heir, she could have had Larry Holland for a husband.''

''Oh,'' Josiah said, looking at Violet with what she considered added respect.

''Well, I can't be worried about that now,'' Violet said. ''I'm getting married in a few hours, and money is my least concern.''

Josiah rose. ''Then I've discharged my duty, so I'll leave now.''

Hesitantly, Violet said, "Would you like to stay for the wedding? You are welcome."

"I had hoped you would ask. I'll be happy to attend."

"And I'll be happy to have you there. Aunt Ruth is the only other relative I have. Six o'clock at First Community Church."

With tender eyes, Violet watched Josiah walk toward his car. "It seems that I won't be able to forget the Conleys, after all," Violet said.

"Who would want to forget a grandmother like her?" Roger responded, as he tapped the letter Violet held. "I believe you inherited more of her characteristics than just the physical features. She must have had a great heart."

"This recognition erases all of the feelings of rejection I had in my childhood. I was loved more than I knew. And I'll admit that I am relieved not to have constraint between my grandfather and me. Regardless of what he did to my mother, I've forgiven him—it's unchristian to do otherwise. I hope this works out all right."

Roger drew her close. "I believe that Josiah is convinced that you will not give in to his demands and that he respects you for it." He smiled and said teasingly, "I believe you inherited a little of Josiah's stubbornness, too. And as far as I'm concerned, there's no need for you to be estranged from him."

As Violet and Misty waited in the church office for the processional to begin, the soloist's rendition of Rodgers and Hammerstein's *You'll Never Walk Alone* wafted into the room.

The soloist sung of the dark days that would come

into each life, but in spite of storms, rain or dashed dreams, the lyrics gave assurance that one need never walk alone.

Violet knew about storms all right—for the past several months it seemed as if she weathered one storm only to be struck by another one, but even in the midst of her most discouraging moments, she hadn't given up hope. She had relied often on a passage from the book of Hebrews, "Hope we have as an anchor of the soul, both sure and steadfast."

What a sense of security! Hand in hand with Roger, and both of them holding God's hand, she *would* never walk alone.

The song ended, and Misty prepared to enter the sanctuary. Violet went to her, straightened the white rose corsage on her shoulder and kissed her on the cheek. Tears glistened in Misty's eyes. "It will be nice to have a mother again. Please make my daddy happy," she whispered.

"I'll do my best, Misty," Violet vowed. "I love him very much."

When Misty stepped out into the hallway, Violet took one last look in the mirror and adjusted Rachel's diamond-and-ruby necklace. The long pendant earrings dangled almost to her shoulders. The jewelry set off her gown to perfection, and today she appreciated this link to her paternal heritage—clouded though it was, she could no longer deny her Conley lineage. Besides, she knew Josiah would be pleased if she wore Rachel's jewels.

Instead of the traditional wedding march, Violet had asked the organist to play the hymn, "Savior, Like a Shepherd Lead Us," as she walked down the aisle—alone. She had never been more conscious of her lack of parents than she was now. A woman should have her mother and father on her wedding day. Perhaps if she had known ahead of time that her grandfather would be there, she might have asked him to give her away, but that could have been too memorable of the time when he rejected her when she was a child. *Stop it!* she mentally chided herself. No morbid thoughts today.

As she walked slowly, the delicate train flowing behind her, Violet looked forward and saw her new family waiting expectantly. Standing proudly by his father, Jason was as handsome as Roger. Misty smiled invitingly, and Violet didn't feel any older than this girl who would soon be her daughter. When they had posed for a family portrait prior to the ceremony, Roger had joked, "People will accuse me of taking another daughter rather than a wife. But having so many children around should restore my youthful vigor."

"As if you have ever lost any," Jason reprimanded his father. "Get serious, Dad."

The aisle looked long, but she knew that when the recessional was played, the aisle would seem short because Roger would walk by her side—she would never be alone again. Their glances held as she walked the few remaining steps. Roger's hand was trembling when he reached for hers, and she gave him a tremulous smile.

Pastor Tom's service was brief, and it seemed a very short time until they were kneeling, hand in hand, listening to the soloist sing "The Lord's Prayer."

Beneath the words of the soloist, Roger prayed quietly, "Lord, we love each other, but we love you more. We will need your daily guidance to be loving, considerate spouses and good parents. We praise you for bringing us together.''

Violet echoed his ''Amen,'' as the soloist finished the song.

The two-hundred-seat sanctuary was filled to capacity, Violet noted as they started down the aisle as man and wife. Janie sat between Clifford and Alta Skeen, all of them smiling, not only for Violet's gladness, but for their own happiness of becoming a family. Josiah sat on the rear seat, and he nodded approvingly as they passed him.

During the reception when Josiah reached the wedding party, he leaned over to kiss Violet's cheek. Tears glistened in his eyes. ''Today has taken me back fifty years,'' he said. ''You are so much like my Rachel. She was beautiful on our wedding day.'' He gently placed a hand on the diamond choker. ''Thanks for wearing that. You wouldn't have known, but Rachel also wore it at our wedding.''

Josiah turned to Roger. ''You've made a fine choice. She looks like her grandmother, and if she has my Rachel's spirit, she will make a wonderful wife.''

''I'll care for her as if she were a rare treasure, and she is one to me,'' Roger said as he returned Josiah's handclasp.

''I have to leave now for I must be back in Kansas City tonight, but you do have my best wishes. I hope you will not cut me off completely, and that I can contact you occasionally.''

Violet looked at Roger, and he responded, ''We're moving into a new home in the Colonial Acres subdivision, and you'll be welcome to visit us at anytime.''

As they watched Josiah's departure, Violet whispered, ''In case I've forgotten to mention it today, I love you very much, Roger.''

''I rather suspected that, but thanks for telling me anyway.''

Once all the guests had passed the receiving line, Violet and Roger went through the ritualistic cutting of the cake, feeding each other a choice bit, and drinking punch arm in arm. When they approached the heavily laden gift table, Ruth intercepted them. She handed Violet an envelope. ''Your grandfather left this for you.''

Violet pulled a $5,000 check out of the envelope. She sighed and handed it to Roger. ''What are we going to do with him? I've made it plain that we don't want his money.''

''Keep it,'' Roger said. ''I figure we will make better use of it than he will. I'll just have to swallow my pride. It isn't your fault you were born a Conley. We've won most of the battles with him, so we'll have to call a compromise on this one.''

''I'd like to do something special with the money. You mentioned once that you'd like to take a tour of the Holy Land. How far would this go toward a tour like that?''

''Probably far enough that we could swing the rest of it ourselves. I like that idea. Before the summer is out, maybe we can have a honeymoon after all.''

After they opened the rest of their gifts, and while their guests were enjoying cake and punch, Roger winked at Violet, and they dodged out the side door of the reception hall. They had acquainted Aunt Ruth and Roger's mother with their wish to leave early, asking them to entertain the guests, and the hospitality committee of the church would take care of any necessary housekeeping activities. No one was watching as Roger opened the door of the pickup and helped Violet enter. Just as they pulled away from the curb, Jason and one of his friends came around the side of the church with tin cans and tubes of shaving cream in their hands.

"Hey," Jason shouted. "That's not fair."

Roger tooted the horn, and Violet waved and laughed at them as they sped down the street.

They hadn't told anyone of their destination, simply that they would be back on the morning of the second day to take his family to the airport—Jason off on his European tour and Misty and her grandmother to Arizona. Roger had taken their clothing to the farm several days ago, so no packing had been necessary.

"Well, Mrs. Gibson," Roger said, "why are you so quiet? Not having second thoughts, are you?"

"I was thinking of the first day you brought me to the farm, and of all the events that have transpired since then. What a difference a few months have made! Then, I didn't have a clue that you loved me. I was estranged from all of my family except Aunt Ruth, and I had an unforgiving spirit toward them. Loving you, and having you return my love, is the most wonderful thing that has happened to me. I've felt alone all my life, and now I not only have you, but you gave me a family as well."

"You've brought happiness into my life, too, and I'm looking forward to our future together."

When Roger parked in front of the small farmhouse, he said, "There's one Scripture that I wish Pastor Tom would have included in the service. Do you remember the words of Ruth in the Old Testament that are often quoted at weddings? Perhaps we could say them to-

gether as the epitome of our mutual commitment.''
They clasped hands and locked glances as they made
the binding promise.

*Where you go I will go, and where you stay I will
stay. Your people will be my people and your God
my God.*

* * * * *

Dear Reader,

Frequently I'm asked, "How long does it take you to write a book?" That's a difficult question to answer, for the time needed to write a book varies with each story.

Probably the best answer would be, "It takes a lifetime to write a book," for whatever a writer produces, either fiction or nonfiction, is a composite of the author's life up to that point. While I have never considered any of my writing as autobiographical, I do rely heavily upon information I've accumulated during years of varied experiences. The ideas for most of my historicals germinated when I was studying and researching for my master's degree in history, or when I was teaching the subject to ninth graders. I was inspired to write my books on early church history while touring Switzerland, Germany and Holland in 1992.

And my interest in writing for the inspirational market has been a result of my religious training from early childhood. Prayer, Bible study and church involvement have been my normal routine for most of my life. Although I've experimented with secular writing, I've had little success, perhaps because God was directing me toward a more fulfilling ministry—inspirational fiction.

It's still an awesome experience when I see a new book in print. I often express my gratitude in the words of David: "Who am I, O Sovereign Lord, and what is my family, that you have brought me this far?" (*II Samuel* 7:18b)

I pray that you will be uplifted spiritually by reading this book. May God bless you.

Irene B. Brand

Love Inspired™

—romance fiction that will lift your spirits!

Welcome to Love Inspired. Each Love Inspired title is a heartwarming, inspiring romance novel where contemporary characters learn the importance of love and faith!

Love Inspired offers a wide range of story types—suspenseful, lighthearted, dramatic and of course romantic! And happy endings are guaranteed!

Look for three brand-new titles every month.

Available wherever Harlequin and Silhouette books are sold.

Love Inspired—
the best in inspirational romance fiction!

Steeple
Hill™

IGEN98

Continuing in February 1999 from Love Inspired®...

SUDDENLY!

Celebrate the joy of unexpected parenthood in this heartwarming series about some very unexpected special deliveries.

SUDDENLY DADDY (June 1998)
SUDDENLY MOMMY (August 1998)

Don't miss the last book in the series...

SUDDENLY MARRIED
by Loree Lough

Noah vowed to keep religion in his children's lives even though he was struggling with his own faith. Then he met Sunday school teacher Dara Mackenzie, who taught his children about their religion, and taught Noah about the healing power of prayer, faith and love.

Don't miss SUDDENLY MARRIED in February 1999 from

 *Love Inspired®*

Available at your favorite retail outlet.

ILISM

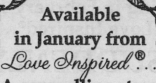

**Available
in January from**
Love Inspired®...
**A compelling story
that will touch your heart...
A book you won't soon forget...**

*A BRIDE
AT LAST*
by *Carolyne Aarsen*

Nadine Laidlaw's search for the truth behind her
father's mysterious death has become an obsession that
threatens to destroy her future with the only man she
has ever loved. Can Nadine find the strength she needs
to put the past to rest?

**Don't miss A BRIDE AT LAST
in January 1999 from**

Love Inspired®

Available at your favorite retail outlet.

ILIABAL

Available in
February 1999
from

Love Inspired ®...

BRIDES AND BLESSINGS

by *Molly Noble Bull*

When Suzann Condry agrees to assume her long-lost twin sister's role as a sweet church librarian, she can't help falling in love with the church's handsome preacher. Will their love survive if she reveals her true identity?

Watch for BRIDES AND BLESSINGS in February 1999 from

 *Love Inspired* ®

Available at your favorite retail outlet.

ILIBAB

Available in February 1999 from
Love Inspired ®...

WEDDING AT WILDWOOD

by *Lenora Worth*

When Isabel Landry returns to her hometown, she is forced to come to terms with the intolerance that forced her to abandon her dreams of being with the man she has always loved.

Watch for WEDDING AT WILDWOOD in February 1999 from

® *Love Inspired* ®

Available at your favorite retail outlet.

ILIWAW